D1479958

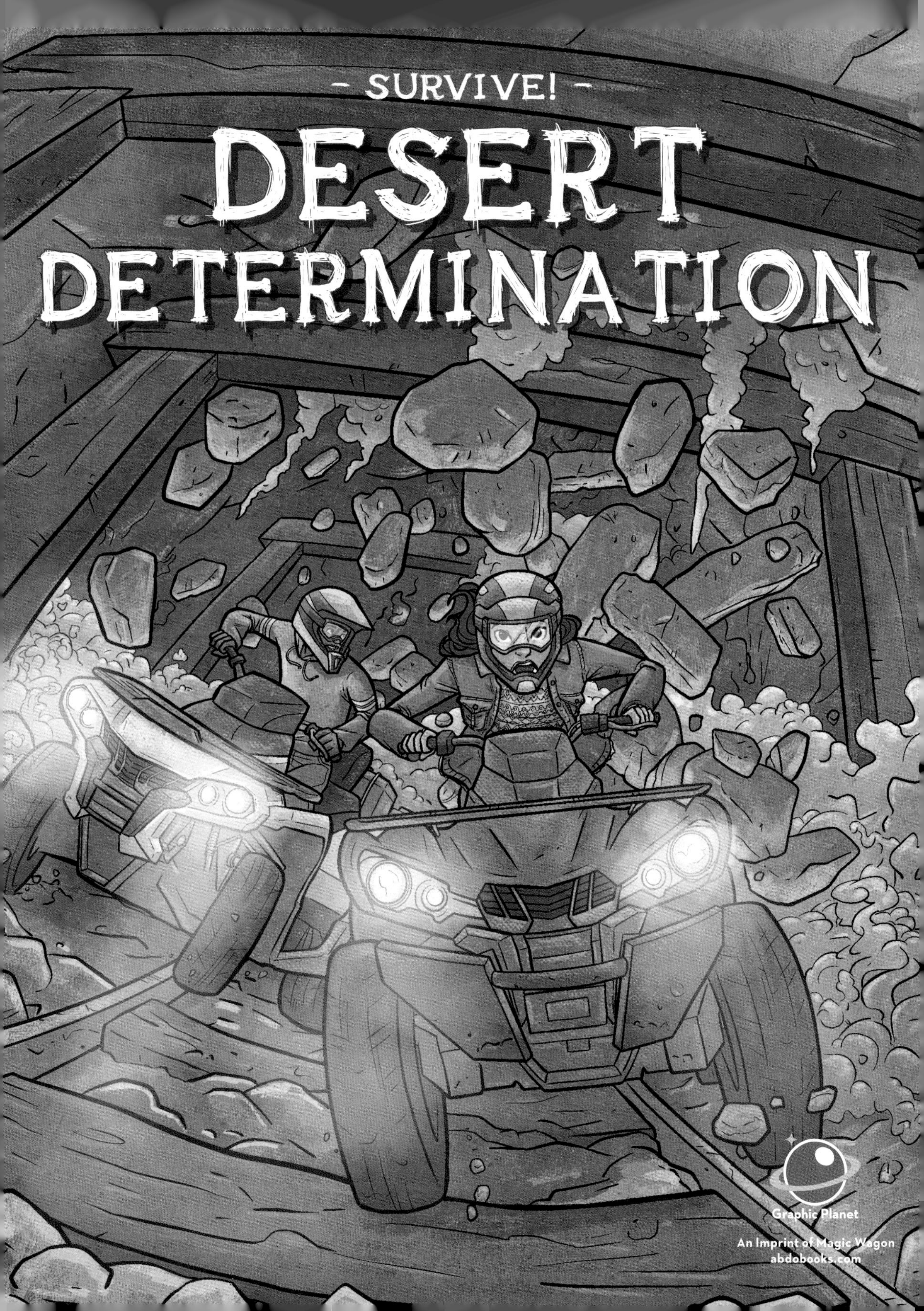
- SURVIVE! -
DESERT
DETERMINATION
Graphic Planet
An Imprint of Magic Wagon
abdobooks.com

abdobooks.com

Published by Magic Wagon, a division of ABDO, PO Box 398166, Minneapolis, Minnesota 55439.
Copyright © 2020 by Abdo Consulting Group, Inc. International copyrights reserved in all countries.
No part of this book may be reproduced in any form without written permission from the publisher.
Graphic Planet™ is a trademark and logo of Magic Wagon.

Printed in the United States of America, North Mankato, Minnesota.
052019
092019

 **THIS BOOK CONTAINS
RECYCLED MATERIALS**

Written by Bill Yu
Illustrated by Thiago Vale and Yonami
Colored by Dal Bello
Lettered by Kathryn S. Renta
Editorial supervision by David Campiti
Packaged by Glass House Graphics
Art Directed by Christina Doffing
Editorial Support by Tamara L. Britton

Library of Congress Control Number: 2018965021

Publisher's Cataloging-in-Publication Data

Names: Yu, Bill, author. |Bello, Dal; Vale, illustrators.
Title: Desert determination / by Bill Yu; illustrated by Dal Bello and Vale.
Description: Minneapolis, Minnesota : Magic Wagon, 2020. | Series: Survive!
Summary: Rob and Lillian's families have vacationed together for years. This year they are on an ATV
    tour in the desert. When they find an abandoned mine they decide to ride in and explore. But then
    a cave-in blocks the way out, leaving them trapped. Can they survive?
Identifiers: ISBN 9781532135118 (lib. bdg.) | ISBN 9781644941393 (pbk.) | ISBN
9781532135712 (ebook) | ISBN 9781532136016 (Read-to-Me ebook)
    Subjects: LCSH: Family vacations--Juvenile fiction. | Spelunking--Juvenile fiction. | Caving--Juvenile
    fiction. | Caving accidents--Juvenile fiction. | Survival skills--Juvenile fiction.
Classification: DDC 741.5--dc23

TABLE OF CONTENTS

True Tales of
Survival

You never know when you'll need outdoor survival skills. Sometimes you'll be prepared, other times you won't!

Water Wisdom

In July of 2012, William LaFever needed to travel from Boulder, Utah, to Page, Arizona. Instead of taking public transportation, he and his dog began a 90-mile (145-km) walk along the Escalante River. Along the way, he ran out of food and his dog ran off. His gear was so heavy that he took it off and abandoned it. William has autism. While that can make other areas of life more challenging, it may have saved his life. Interestingly, people with autism are often drawn to and calmed by water due to the sensory stimulation it can provide. William stayed near the river, ate frogs, and had a source of hydration and cooling. By chance, the county sheriff had recently completed a course on finding missing people who have autism. He knew that there was a chance William could be attracted to the water. A helicopter searched the area, and found him. William was starving and exhausted after three weeks in the desert. But he was alive!

Desert Adventure

In April of 2012, Victoria Grover was hiking in Utah's Box Death Hollow Wilderness when she broke her leg jumping from a small rock ledge. She was unable to walk and had to scoot in a seated position using her feet and bottom. She had no food and type 2 diabetes. At night, the temperature dropped close to freezing. Worst of all, she hadn't told anyone where she was going! Fortunately, Victoria had taken a wilderness survival course. She knew to make a splint by tying her walking stick to her leg with a scarf. She slept during the daytime heat and kept moving during the cooler night. She was fine for two days. On the third day, she almost died from hypothermia. She was found on the fourth day. Had she not been found, she likely would've died after 96 hours in the desert!

Ghost Town Breakdown

In July of 2017, Mick Ohman was taking a road trip to the Arizona ghost town of Crown King. His car broke down near the Bradshaw Mountains. There was no cell phone service. He had no shelter, and little to eat or drink. Mick left a note on his vehicle and started off to find help. During the hike, he ran out of food and drink. He survived by hydrating himself with water from creeks and his own body fluids. After wandering in the desert for almost three days, he found a man riding a dirt bike! He got a ride back to civilization, received medical treatment, and was taken home.

DESERT DETERMINATION

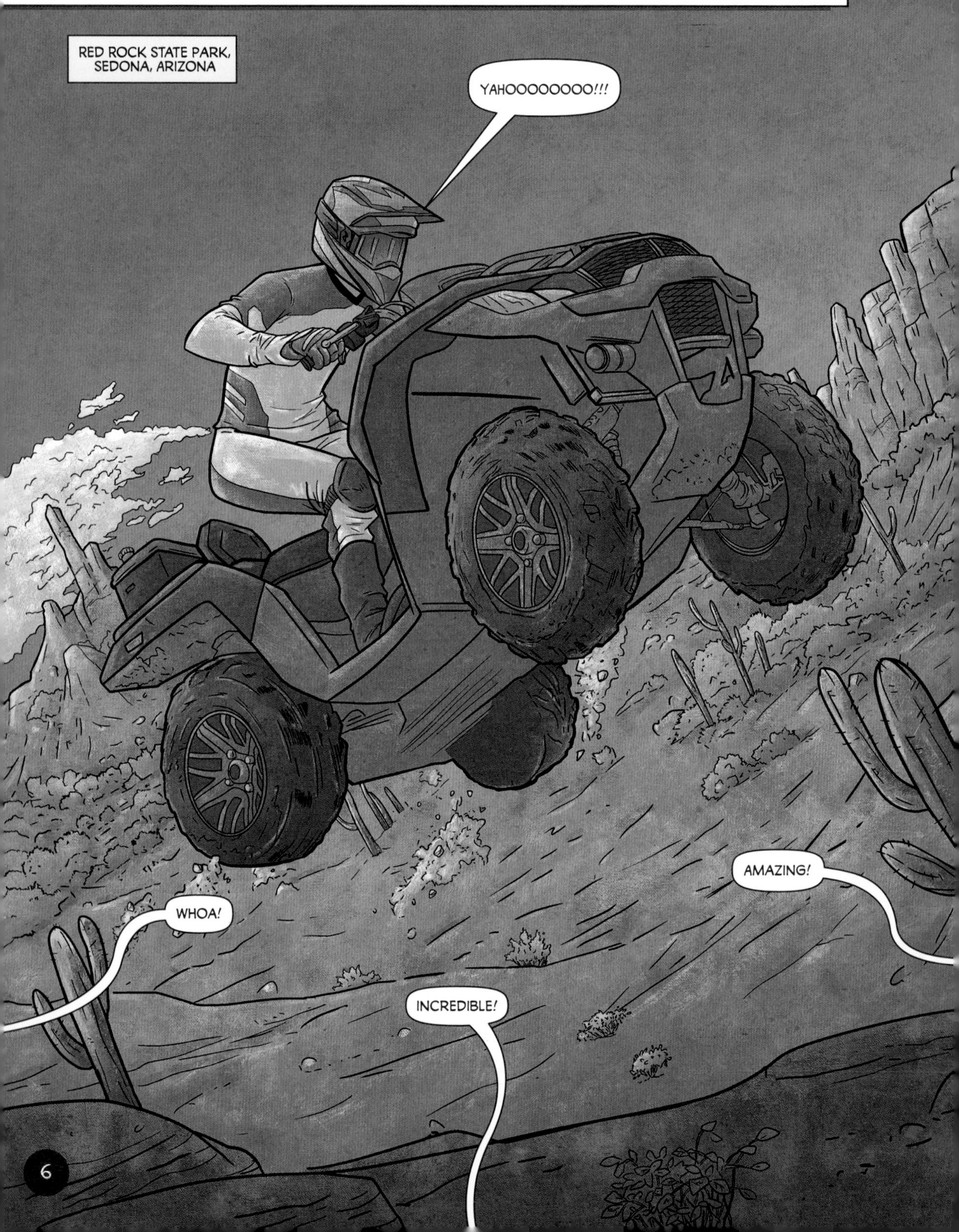

RED ROCK STATE PARK, SEDONA, ARIZONA
YAHOOOOOOOO!!!
WHOA!
AMAZING!
INCREDIBLE!

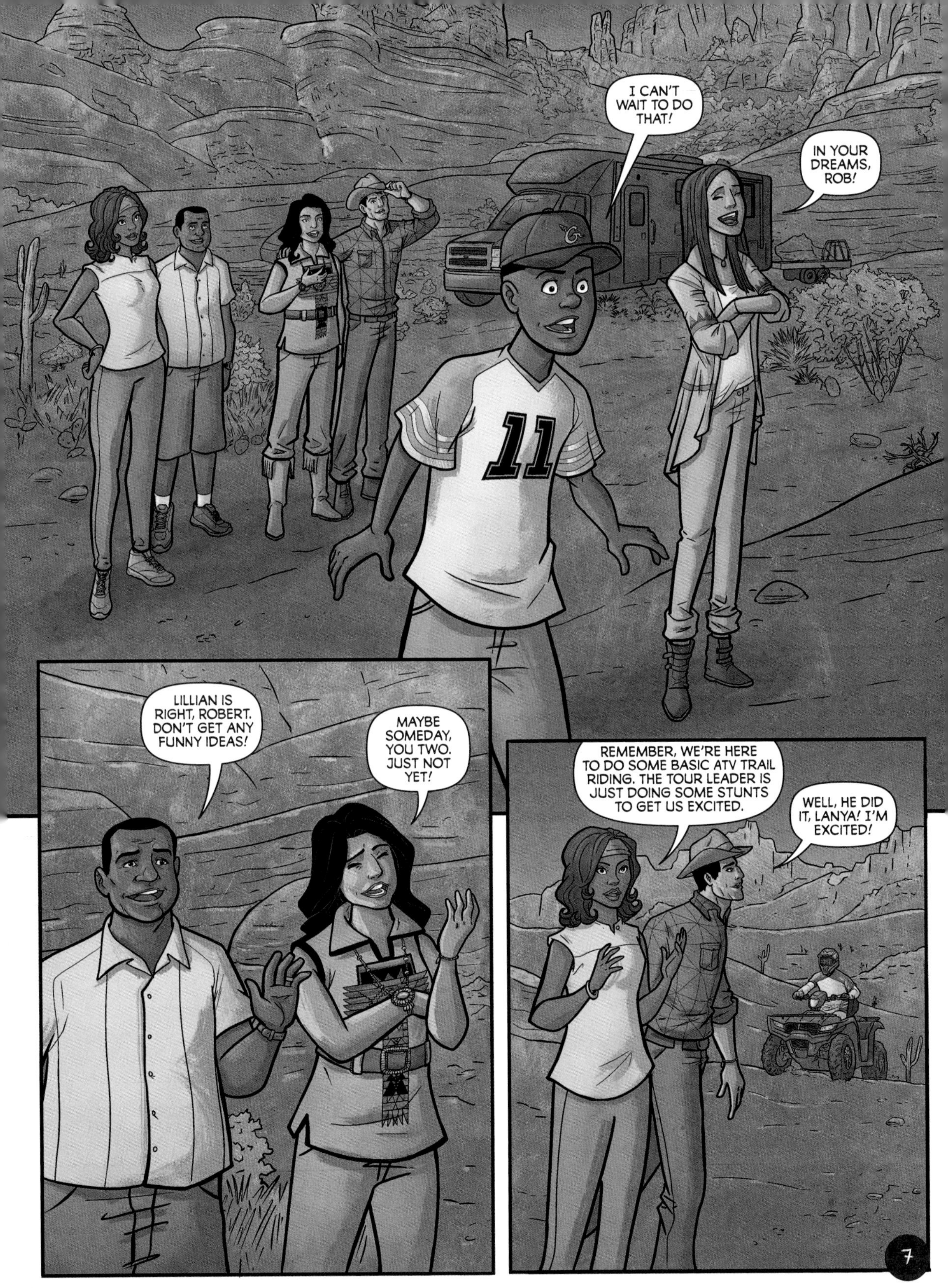
I CAN'T WAIT TO DO THAT!
IN YOUR DREAMS, ROB!
LILLIAN IS RIGHT, ROBERT. DON'T GET ANY FUNNY IDEAS!
MAYBE SOMEDAY, YOU TWO. JUST NOT YET!
REMEMBER, WE'RE HERE TO DO SOME BASIC ATV TRAIL RIDING. THE TOUR LEADER IS JUST DOING SOME STUNTS TO GET US EXCITED.
WELL, HE DID IT, LANYA! I'M EXCITED!

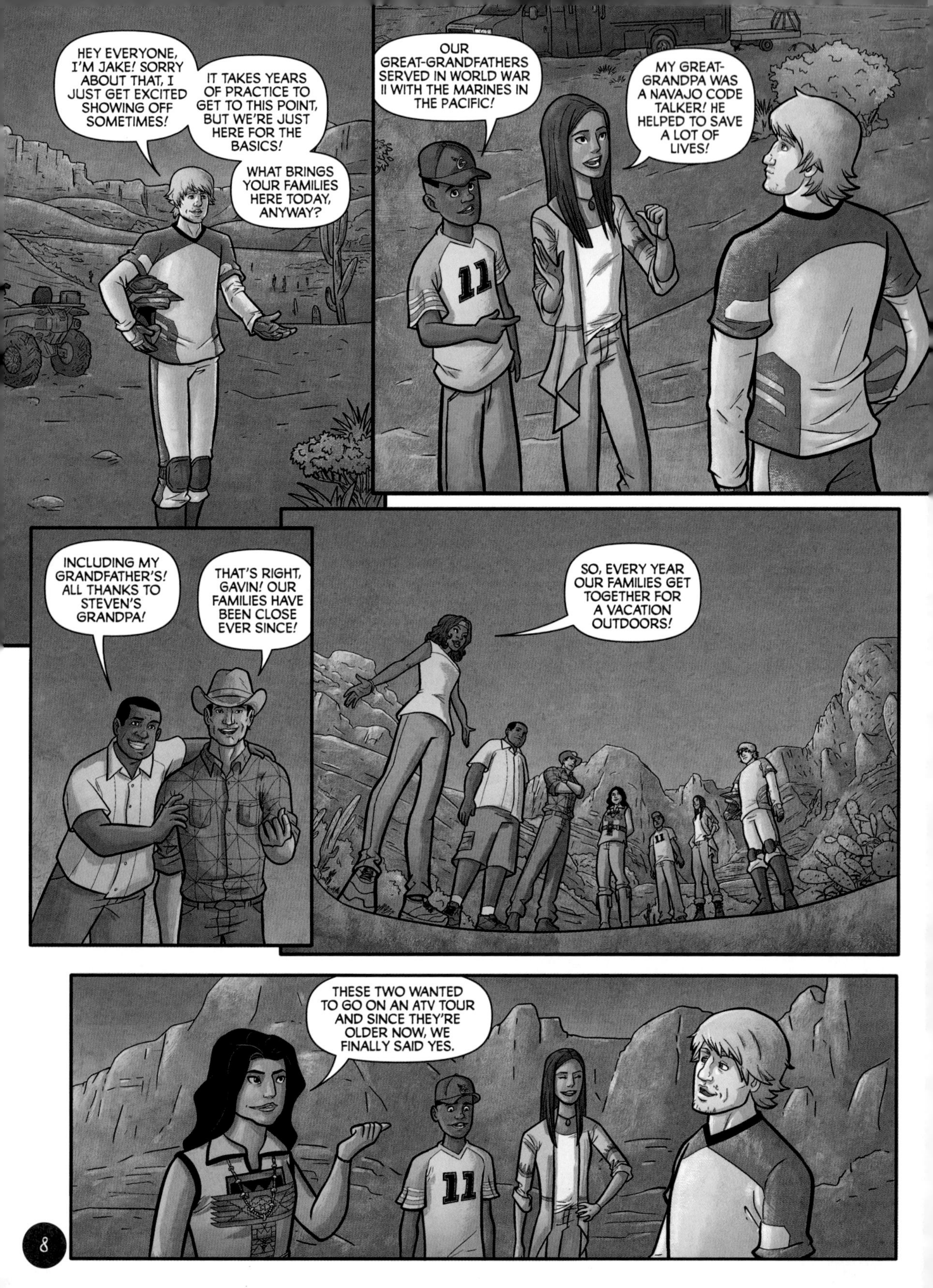
HEY EVERYONE, I'M JAKE! SORRY ABOUT THAT, I JUST GET EXCITED SHOWING OFF SOMETIMES!
IT TAKES YEARS OF PRACTICE TO GET TO THIS POINT, BUT WE'RE JUST HERE FOR THE BASICS!
WHAT BRINGS YOUR FAMILIES HERE TODAY, ANYWAY?
OUR GREAT-GRANDFATHERS SERVED IN WORLD WAR II WITH THE MARINES IN THE PACIFIC!
MY GREAT-GRANDPA WAS A NAVAJO CODE TALKER! HE HELPED TO SAVE A LOT OF LIVES!
INCLUDING MY GRANDFATHER'S! ALL THANKS TO STEVEN'S GRANDPA!
THAT'S RIGHT, GAVIN! OUR FAMILIES HAVE BEEN CLOSE EVER SINCE!
SO, EVERY YEAR OUR FAMILIES GET TOGETHER FOR A VACATION OUTDOORS!
THESE TWO WANTED TO GO ON AN ATV TOUR AND SINCE THEY'RE OLDER NOW, WE FINALLY SAID YES.

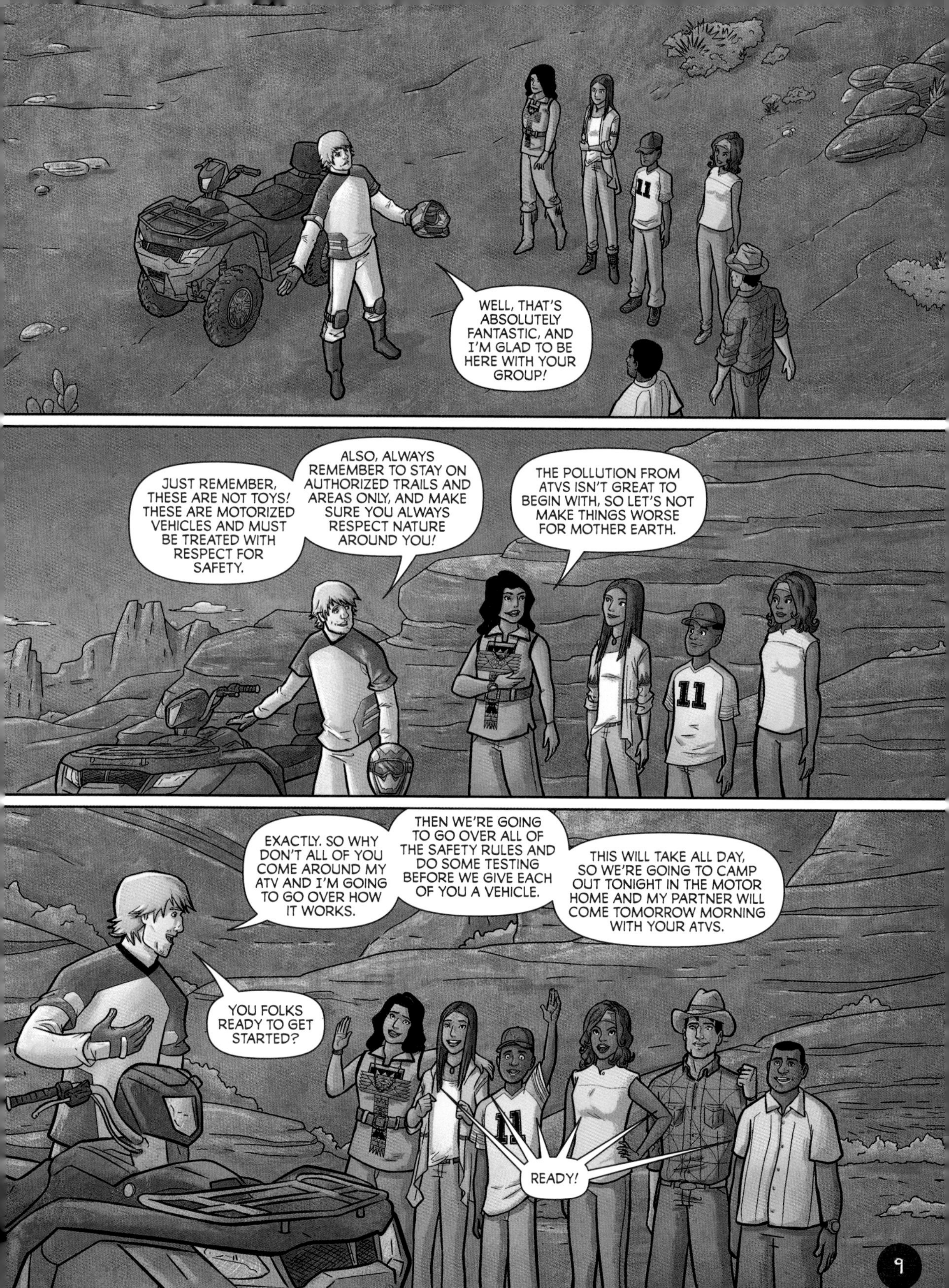
WELL, THAT'S ABSOLUTELY FANTASTIC, AND I'M GLAD TO BE HERE WITH YOUR GROUP!
JUST REMEMBER, THESE ARE NOT TOYS! THESE ARE MOTORIZED VEHICLES AND MUST BE TREATED WITH RESPECT FOR SAFETY.
ALSO, ALWAYS REMEMBER TO STAY ON AUTHORIZED TRAILS AND AREAS ONLY, AND MAKE SURE YOU ALWAYS RESPECT NATURE AROUND YOU!
THE POLLUTION FROM ATVS ISN'T GREAT TO BEGIN WITH, SO LET'S NOT MAKE THINGS WORSE FOR MOTHER EARTH.
EXACTLY. SO WHY DON'T ALL OF YOU COME AROUND MY ATV AND I'M GOING TO GO OVER HOW IT WORKS.
THEN WE'RE GOING TO GO OVER ALL OF THE SAFETY RULES AND DO SOME TESTING BEFORE WE GIVE EACH OF YOU A VEHICLE.
THIS WILL TAKE ALL DAY, SO WE'RE GOING TO CAMP OUT TONIGHT IN THE MOTOR HOME AND MY PARTNER WILL COME TOMORROW MORNING WITH YOUR ATVS.
YOU FOLKS READY TO GET STARTED?
READY!

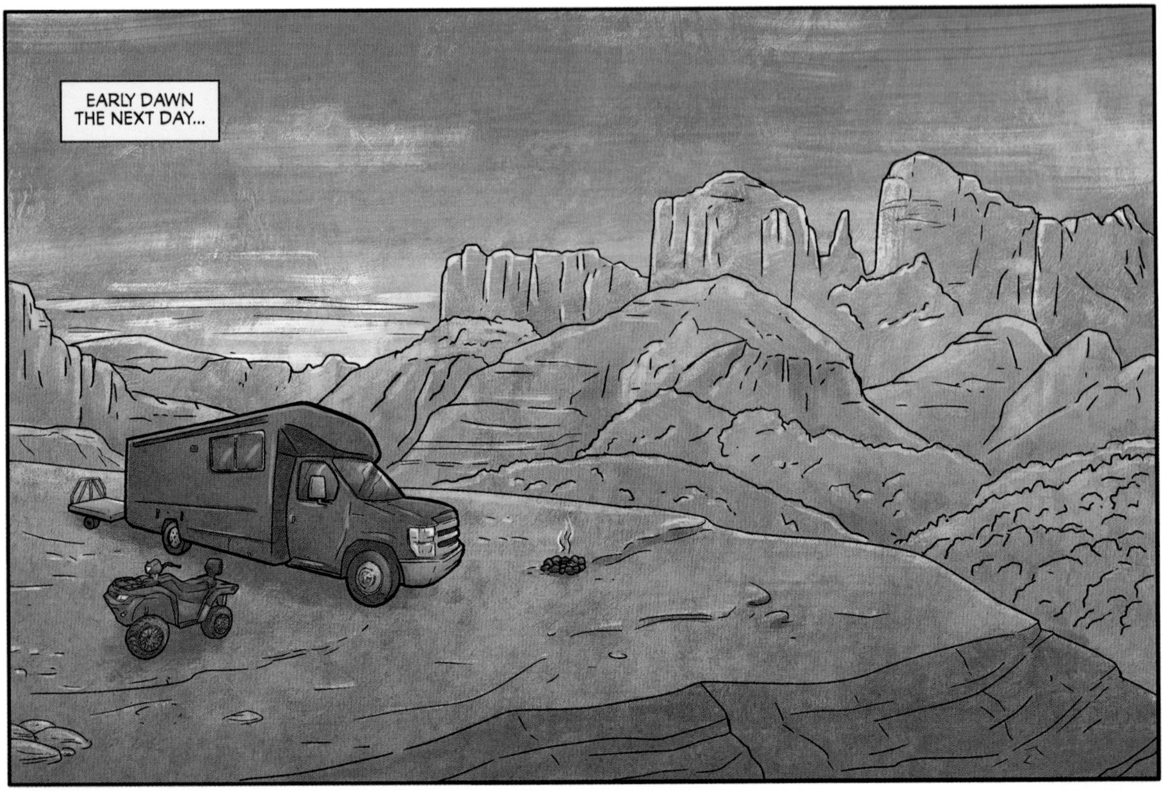
EARLY DAWN
THE NEXT DAY...

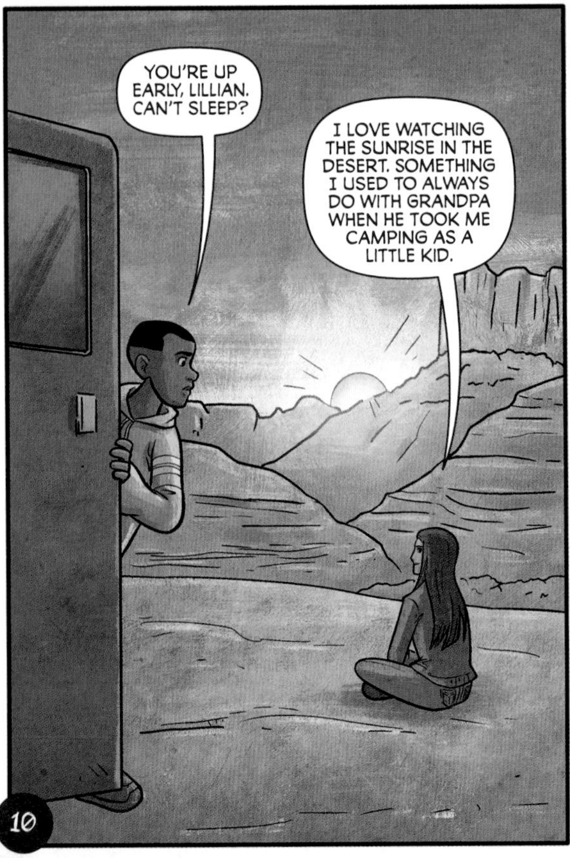
YOU'RE UP EARLY, LILLIAN. CAN'T SLEEP?
I LOVE WATCHING THE SUNRISE IN THE DESERT. SOMETHING I USED TO ALWAYS DO WITH GRANDPA WHEN HE TOOK ME CAMPING AS A LITTLE KID.

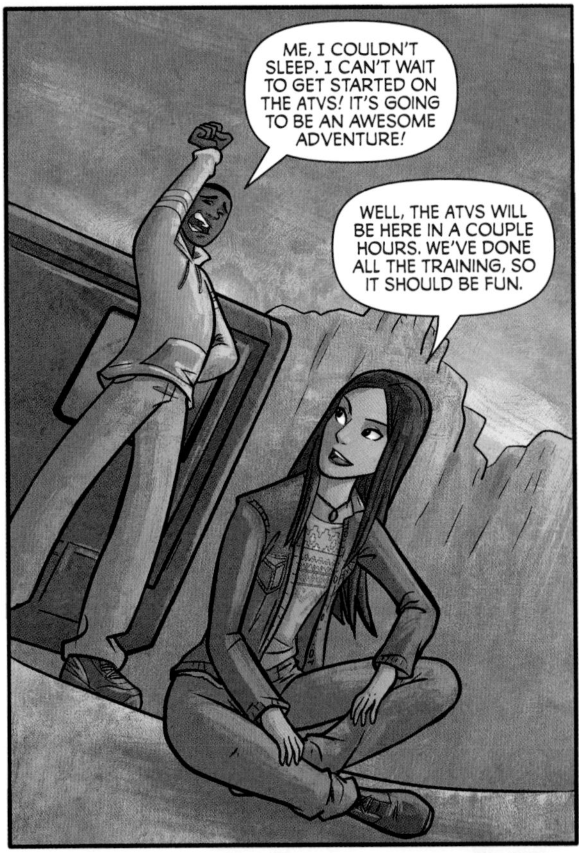
ME, I COULDN'T SLEEP. I CAN'T WAIT TO GET STARTED ON THE ATVS! IT'S GOING TO BE AN AWESOME ADVENTURE!
WELL, THE ATVS WILL BE HERE IN A COUPLE HOURS. WE'VE DONE ALL THE TRAINING, SO IT SHOULD BE FUN.

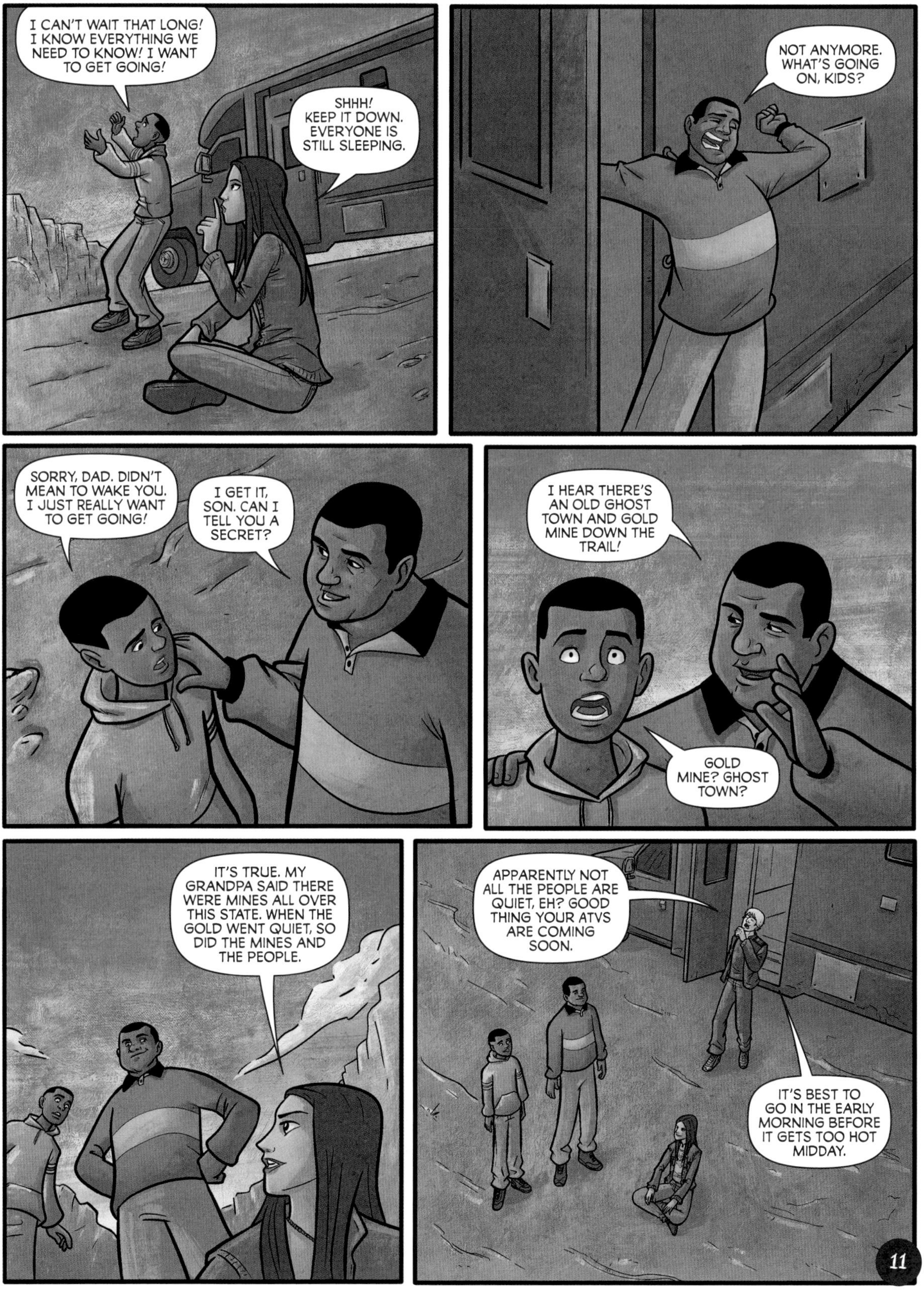

I CAN'T WAIT THAT LONG! I KNOW EVERYTHING WE NEED TO KNOW! I WANT TO GET GOING!
SHHH! KEEP IT DOWN. EVERYONE IS STILL SLEEPING.
NOT ANYMORE. WHAT'S GOING ON, KIDS?
SORRY, DAD. DIDN'T MEAN TO WAKE YOU. I JUST REALLY WANT TO GET GOING!
I GET IT, SON. CAN I TELL YOU A SECRET?
I HEAR THERE'S AN OLD GHOST TOWN AND GOLD MINE DOWN THE TRAIL!
GOLD MINE? GHOST TOWN?
IT'S TRUE. MY GRANDPA SAID THERE WERE MINES ALL OVER THIS STATE. WHEN THE GOLD WENT QUIET, SO DID THE MINES AND THE PEOPLE.
APPARENTLY NOT ALL THE PEOPLE ARE QUIET, EH? GOOD THING YOUR ATVS ARE COMING SOON.
IT'S BEST TO GO IN THE EARLY MORNING BEFORE IT GETS TOO HOT MIDDAY.

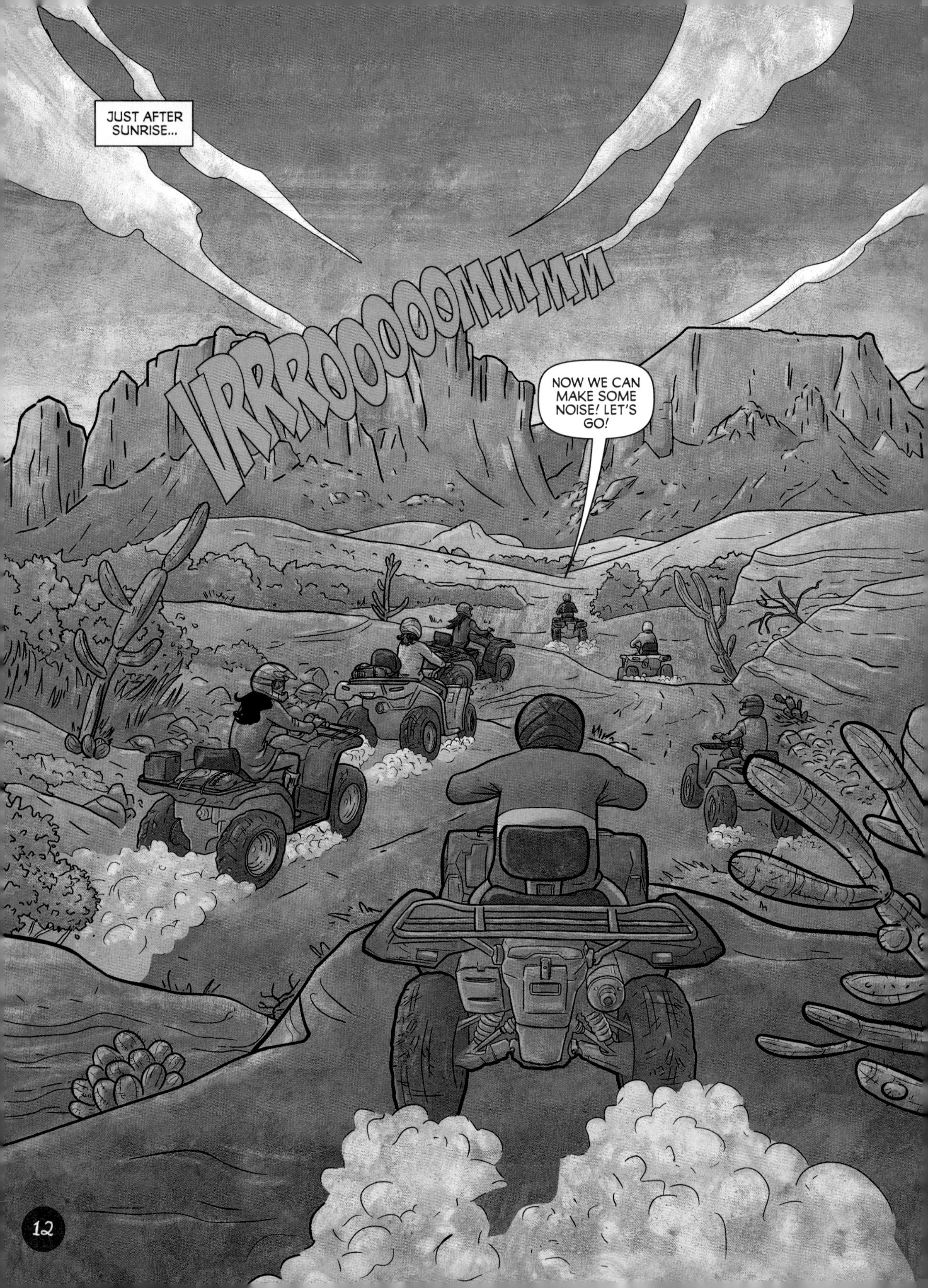
JUST AFTER SUNRISE...
VRRROOOOOMMMMM
NOW WE CAN MAKE SOME NOISE! LET'S GO!

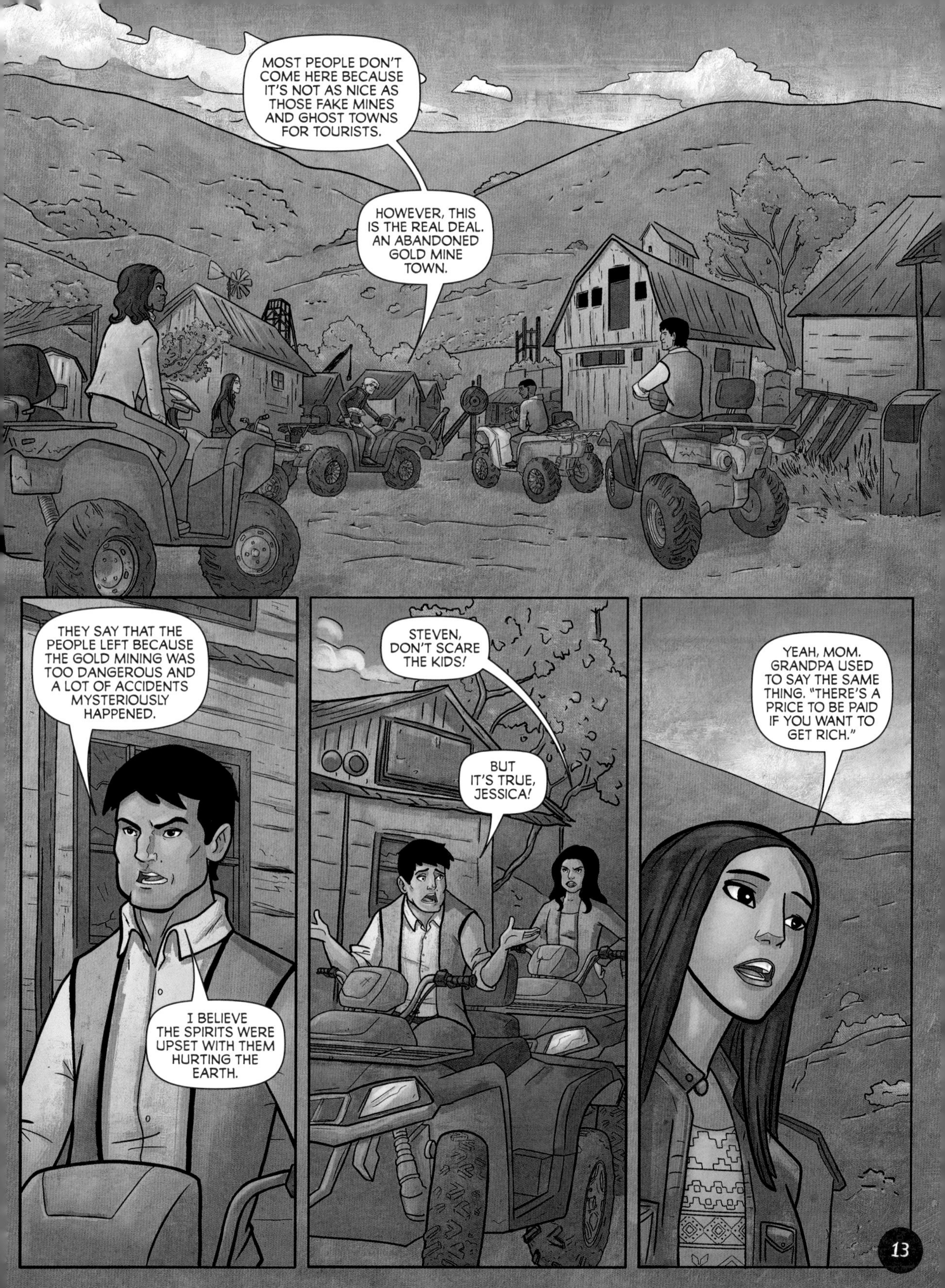
MOST PEOPLE DON'T COME HERE BECAUSE IT'S NOT AS NICE AS THOSE FAKE MINES AND GHOST TOWNS FOR TOURISTS.
HOWEVER, THIS IS THE REAL DEAL. AN ABANDONED GOLD MINE TOWN.
THEY SAY THAT THE PEOPLE LEFT BECAUSE THE GOLD MINING WAS TOO DANGEROUS AND A LOT OF ACCIDENTS MYSTERIOUSLY HAPPENED.
I BELIEVE THE SPIRITS WERE UPSET WITH THEM HURTING THE EARTH.
STEVEN, DON'T SCARE THE KIDS!
BUT IT'S TRUE, JESSICA!
YEAH, MOM. GRANDPA USED TO SAY THE SAME THING. "THERE'S A PRICE TO BE PAID IF YOU WANT TO GET RICH."

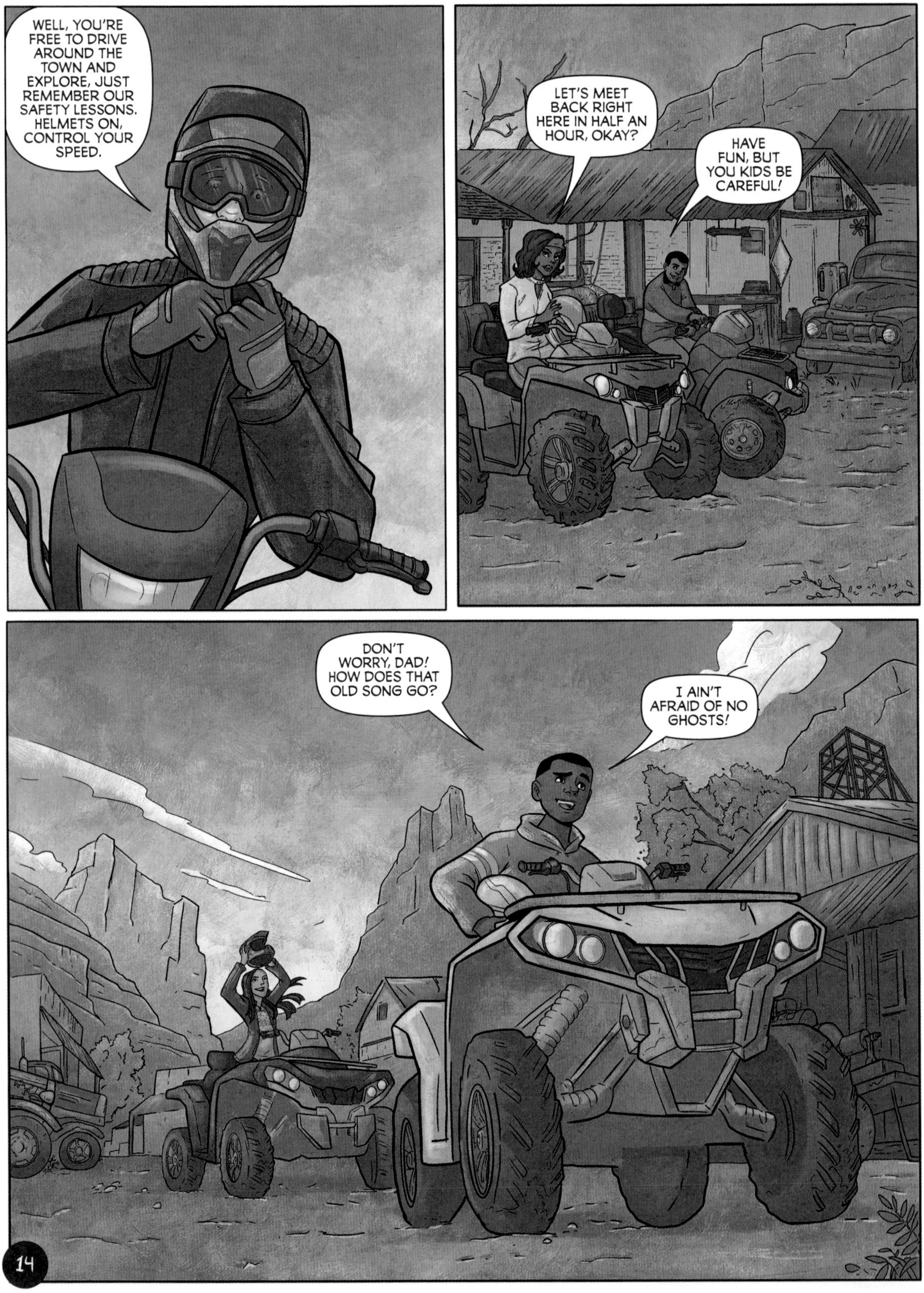

WELL, YOU'RE FREE TO DRIVE AROUND THE TOWN AND EXPLORE, JUST REMEMBER OUR SAFETY LESSONS. HELMETS ON, CONTROL YOUR SPEED.
LET'S MEET BACK RIGHT HERE IN HALF AN HOUR, OKAY?
HAVE FUN, BUT YOU KIDS BE CAREFUL!
DON'T WORRY, DAD! HOW DOES THAT OLD SONG GO?
I AIN'T AFRAID OF NO GHOSTS!

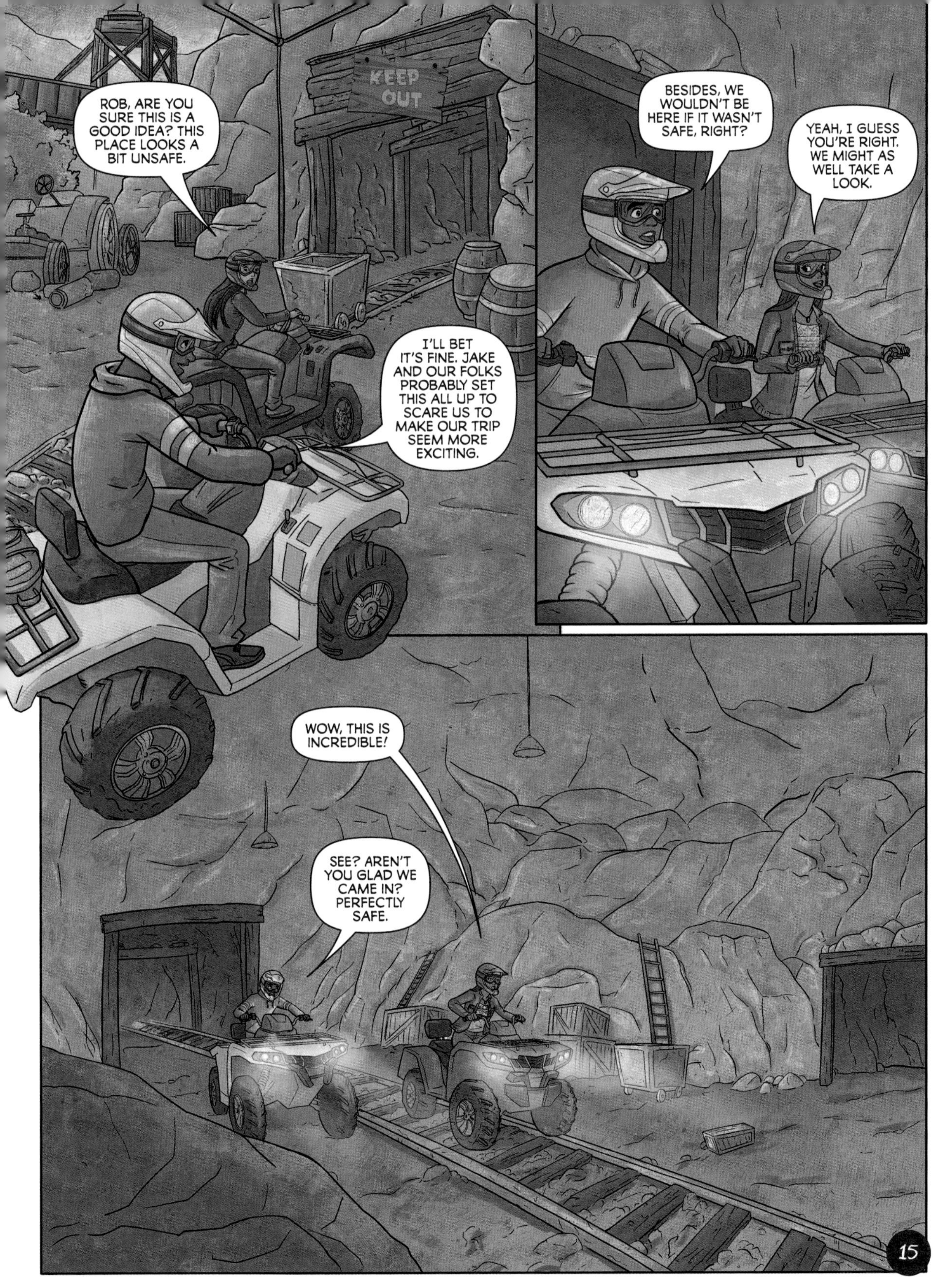
KEEP OUT
ROB, ARE YOU SURE THIS IS A GOOD IDEA? THIS PLACE LOOKS A BIT UNSAFE.
I'LL BET IT'S FINE. JAKE AND OUR FOLKS PROBABLY SET THIS ALL UP TO SCARE US TO MAKE OUR TRIP SEEM MORE EXCITING.
BESIDES, WE WOULDN'T BE HERE IF IT WASN'T SAFE, RIGHT?
YEAH, I GUESS YOU'RE RIGHT. WE MIGHT AS WELL TAKE A LOOK.
WOW, THIS IS INCREDIBLE!
SEE? AREN'T YOU GLAD WE CAME IN? PERFECTLY SAFE.

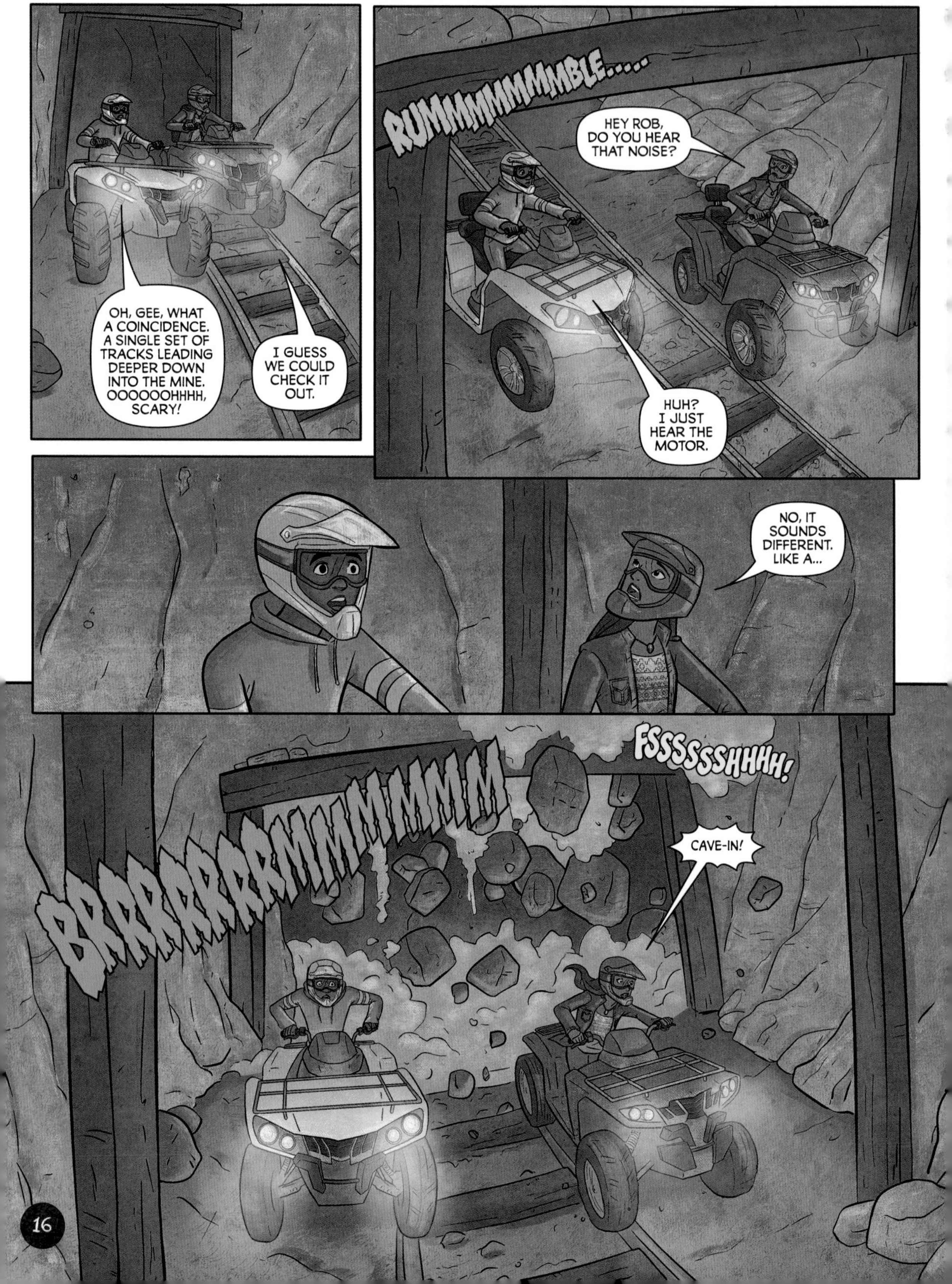

OH, GEE, WHAT A COINCIDENCE. A SINGLE SET OF TRACKS LEADING DEEPER DOWN INTO THE MINE. OOOOOOHHHH, SCARY!
I GUESS WE COULD CHECK IT OUT.
RUMMMMMMMMBLE.....
HEY ROB, DO YOU HEAR THAT NOISE?
HUH? I JUST HEAR THE MOTOR.
NO, IT SOUNDS DIFFERENT. LIKE A...
FSSSSSSHHHH!
BRRRRRRRMMMMMMMM
CAVE-IN!

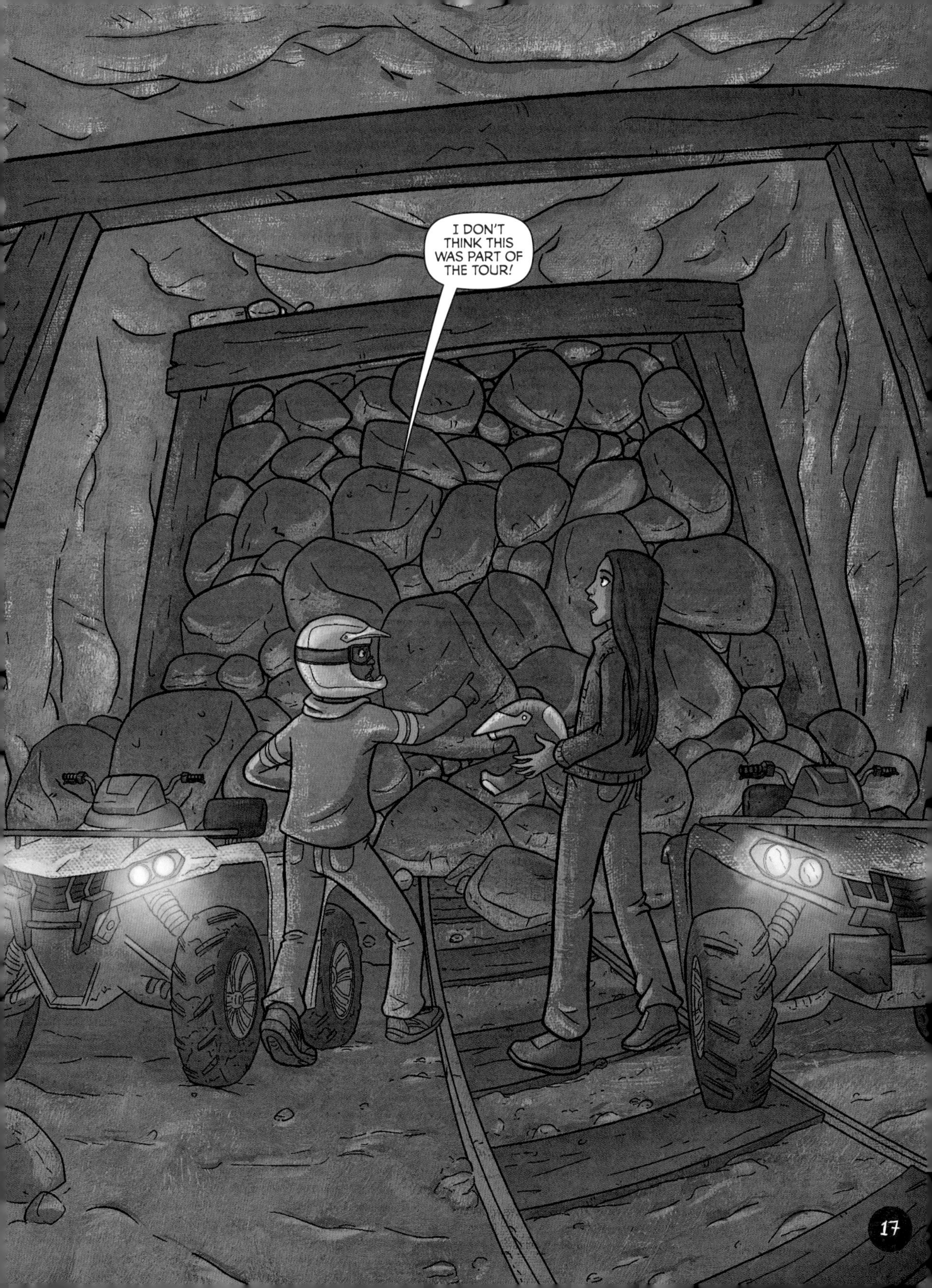
I DON'T THINK THIS WAS PART OF THE TOUR!

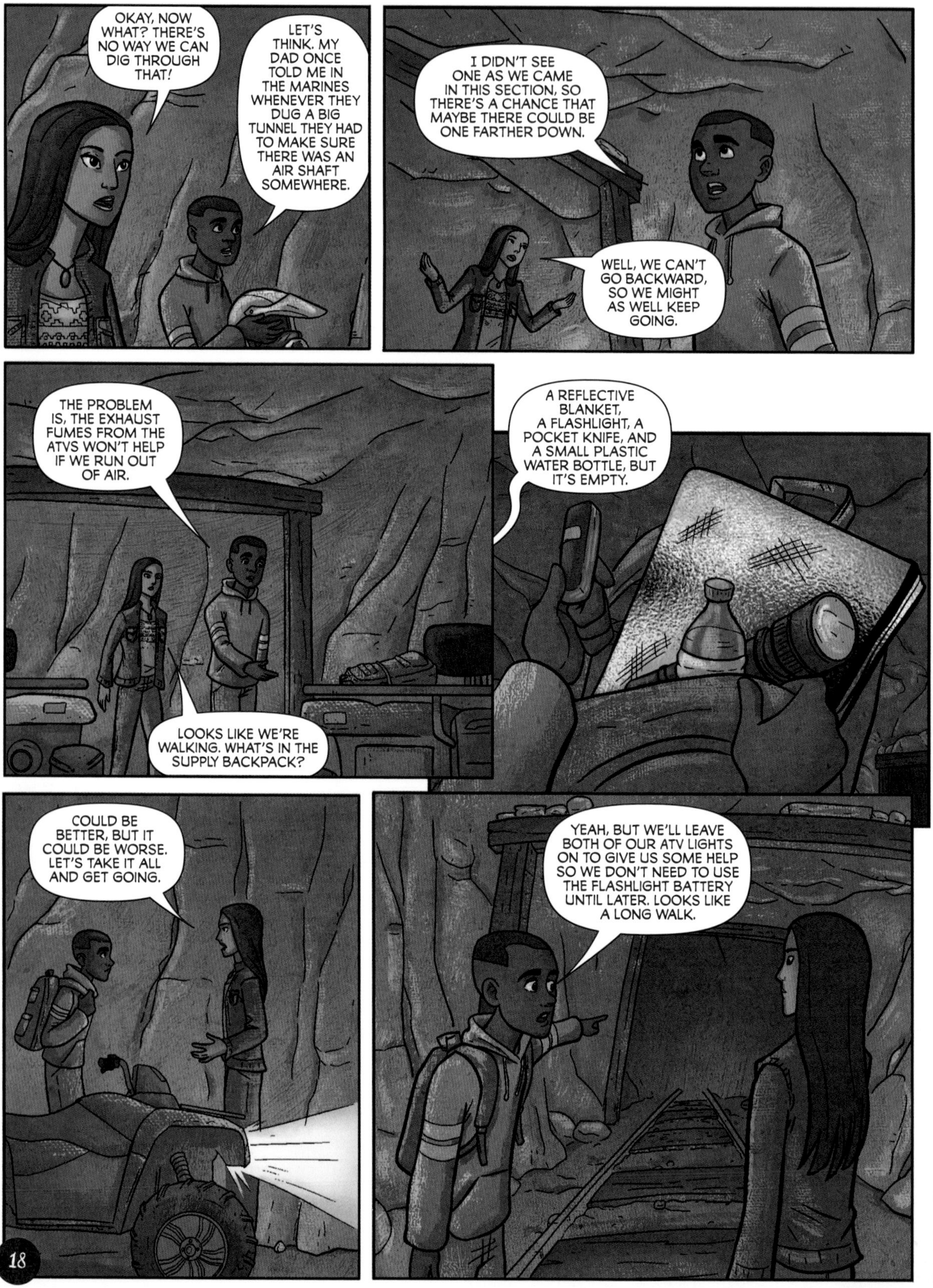
OKAY, NOW WHAT? THERE'S NO WAY WE CAN DIG THROUGH THAT!
LET'S THINK. MY DAD ONCE TOLD ME IN THE MARINES WHENEVER THEY DUG A BIG TUNNEL THEY HAD TO MAKE SURE THERE WAS AN AIR SHAFT SOMEWHERE.
I DIDN'T SEE ONE AS WE CAME IN THIS SECTION, SO THERE'S A CHANCE THAT MAYBE THERE COULD BE ONE FARTHER DOWN.
WELL, WE CAN'T GO BACKWARD, SO WE MIGHT AS WELL KEEP GOING.
THE PROBLEM IS, THE EXHAUST FUMES FROM THE ATVS WON'T HELP IF WE RUN OUT OF AIR.
LOOKS LIKE WE'RE WALKING. WHAT'S IN THE SUPPLY BACKPACK?
A REFLECTIVE BLANKET, A FLASHLIGHT, A POCKET KNIFE, AND A SMALL PLASTIC WATER BOTTLE, BUT IT'S EMPTY.
COULD BE BETTER, BUT IT COULD BE WORSE. LET'S TAKE IT ALL AND GET GOING.
YEAH, BUT WE'LL LEAVE BOTH OF OUR ATV LIGHTS ON TO GIVE US SOME HELP SO WE DON'T NEED TO USE THE FLASHLIGHT BATTERY UNTIL LATER. LOOKS LIKE A LONG WALK.

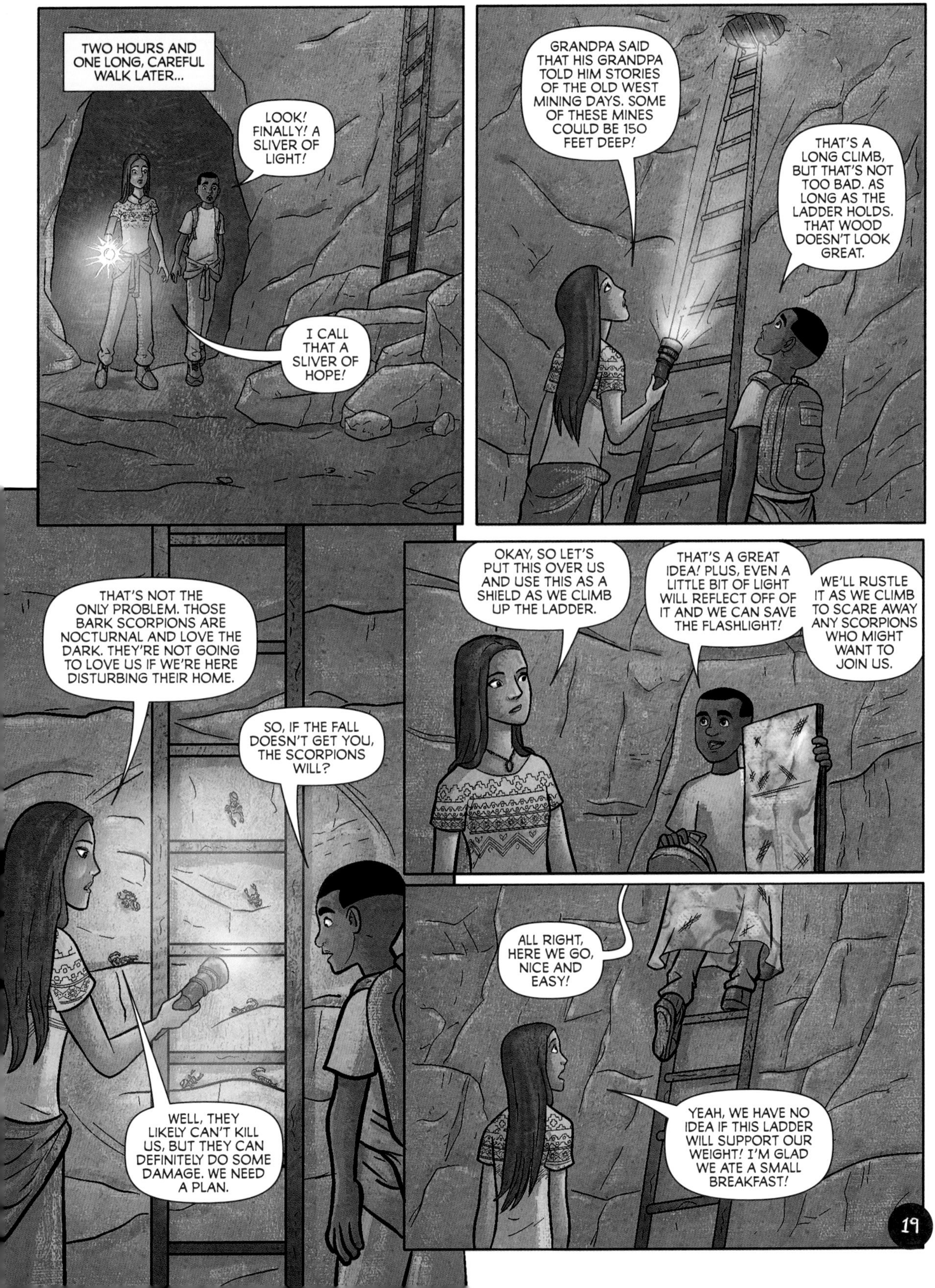
TWO HOURS AND ONE LONG, CAREFUL WALK LATER...
LOOK! FINALLY! A SLIVER OF LIGHT!
I CALL THAT A SLIVER OF HOPE!
GRANDPA SAID THAT HIS GRANDPA TOLD HIM STORIES OF THE OLD WEST MINING DAYS. SOME OF THESE MINES COULD BE 150 FEET DEEP!
THAT'S A LONG CLIMB, BUT THAT'S NOT TOO BAD. AS LONG AS THE LADDER HOLDS. THAT WOOD DOESN'T LOOK GREAT.
THAT'S NOT THE ONLY PROBLEM. THOSE BARK SCORPIONS ARE NOCTURNAL AND LOVE THE DARK. THEY'RE NOT GOING TO LOVE US IF WE'RE HERE DISTURBING THEIR HOME.
SO, IF THE FALL DOESN'T GET YOU, THE SCORPIONS WILL?
WELL, THEY LIKELY CAN'T KILL US, BUT THEY CAN DEFINITELY DO SOME DAMAGE. WE NEED A PLAN.
OKAY, SO LET'S PUT THIS OVER US AND USE THIS AS A SHIELD AS WE CLIMB UP THE LADDER.
THAT'S A GREAT IDEA! PLUS, EVEN A LITTLE BIT OF LIGHT WILL REFLECT OFF OF IT AND WE CAN SAVE THE FLASHLIGHT!
WE'LL RUSTLE IT AS WE CLIMB TO SCARE AWAY ANY SCORPIONS WHO MIGHT WANT TO JOIN US.
ALL RIGHT, HERE WE GO, NICE AND EASY!
YEAH, WE HAVE NO IDEA IF THIS LADDER WILL SUPPORT OUR WEIGHT! I'M GLAD WE ATE A SMALL BREAKFAST!

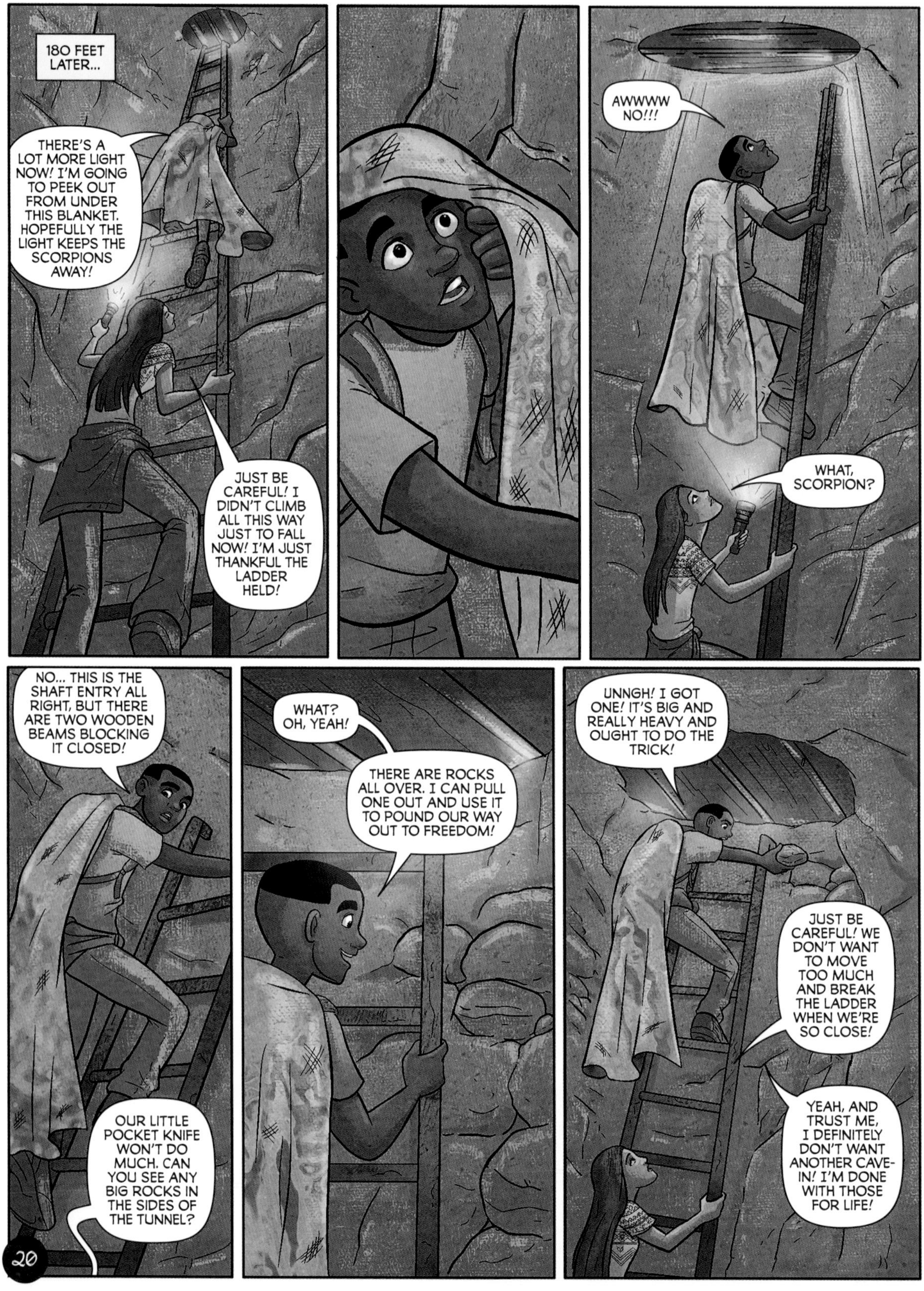
180 FEET LATER...
THERE'S A LOT MORE LIGHT NOW! I'M GOING TO PEEK OUT FROM UNDER THIS BLANKET. HOPEFULLY THE LIGHT KEEPS THE SCORPIONS AWAY!
JUST BE CAREFUL! I DIDN'T CLIMB ALL THIS WAY JUST TO FALL NOW! I'M JUST THANKFUL THE LADDER HELD!
AWWWW NO!!!
WHAT, SCORPION?
NO... THIS IS THE SHAFT ENTRY ALL RIGHT, BUT THERE ARE TWO WOODEN BEAMS BLOCKING IT CLOSED!
OUR LITTLE POCKET KNIFE WON'T DO MUCH. CAN YOU SEE ANY BIG ROCKS IN THE SIDES OF THE TUNNEL?
WHAT? OH, YEAH!
THERE ARE ROCKS ALL OVER. I CAN PULL ONE OUT AND USE IT TO POUND OUR WAY OUT TO FREEDOM!
UNNGH! I GOT ONE! IT'S BIG AND REALLY HEAVY AND OUGHT TO DO THE TRICK!
JUST BE CAREFUL! WE DON'T WANT TO MOVE TOO MUCH AND BREAK THE LADDER WHEN WE'RE SO CLOSE!
YEAH, AND TRUST ME, I DEFINITELY DON'T WANT ANOTHER CAVE-IN! I'M DONE WITH THOSE FOR LIFE!

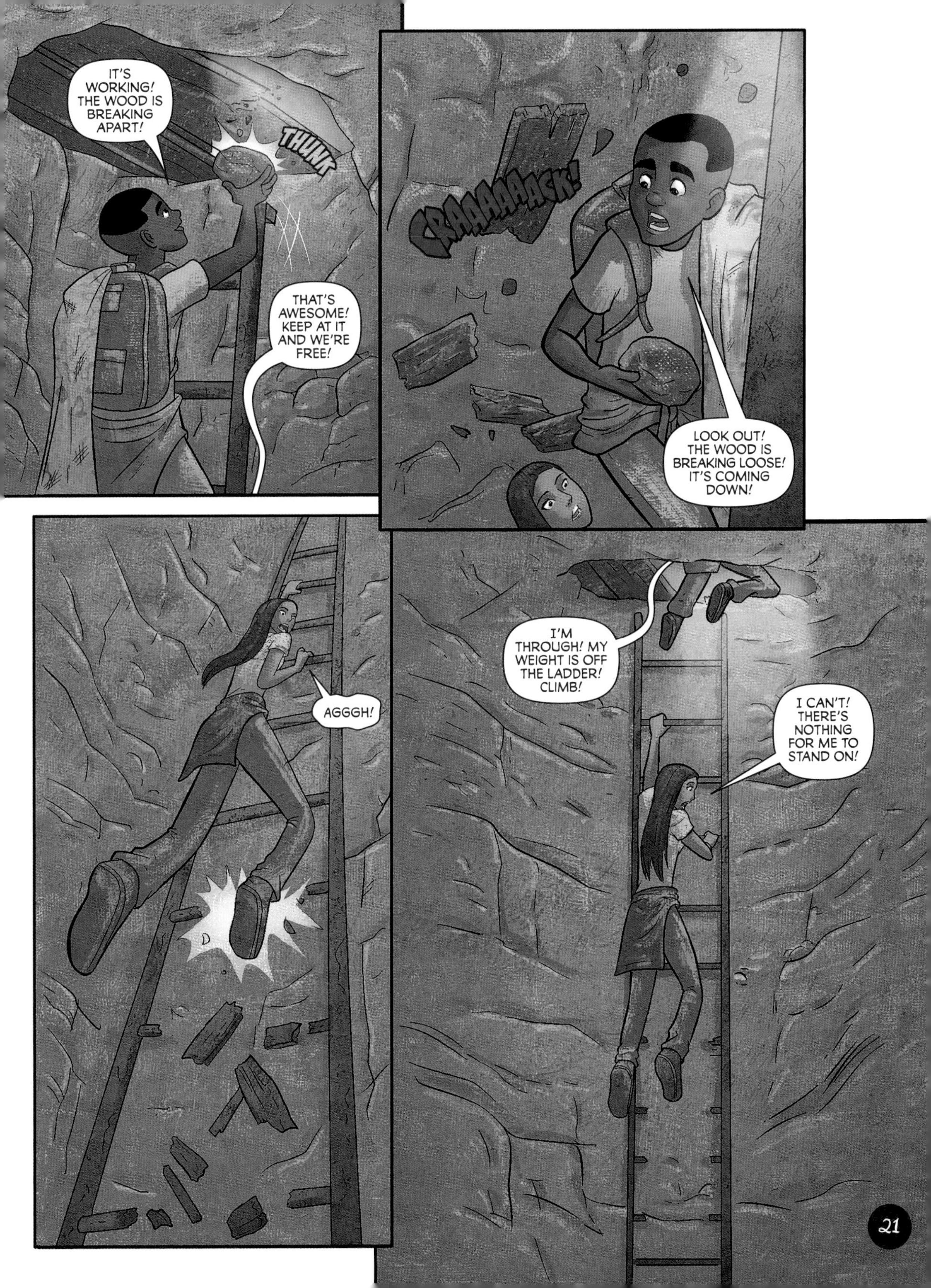
IT'S WORKING! THE WOOD IS BREAKING APART!
THUNK
THAT'S AWESOME! KEEP AT IT AND WE'RE FREE!
CRAAAAAACK!
LOOK OUT! THE WOOD IS BREAKING LOOSE! IT'S COMING DOWN!
AGGGH!
I'M THROUGH! MY WEIGHT IS OFF THE LADDER! CLIMB!
I CAN'T! THERE'S NOTHING FOR ME TO STAND ON!

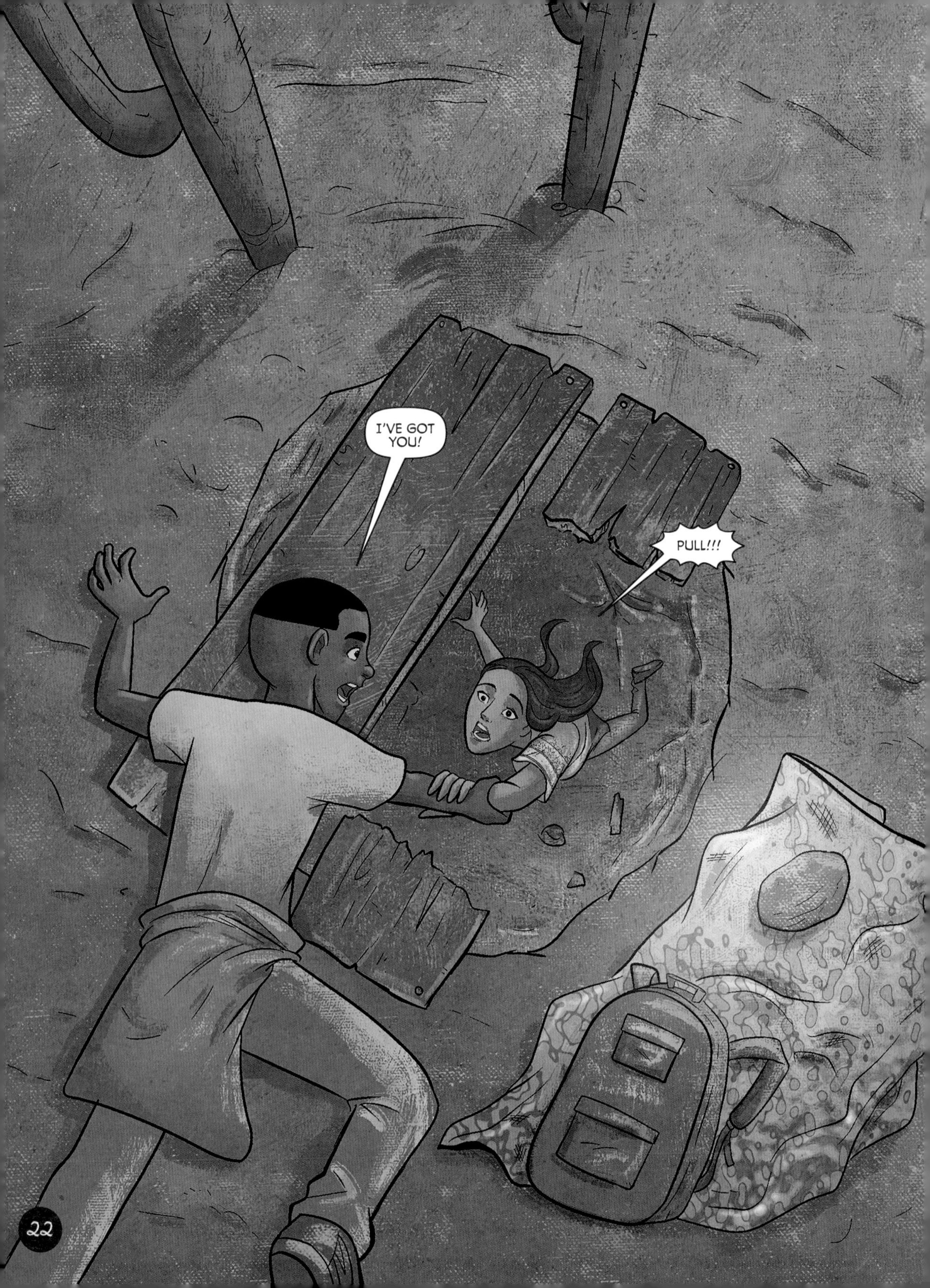
I'VE GOT YOU!
PULL!!!

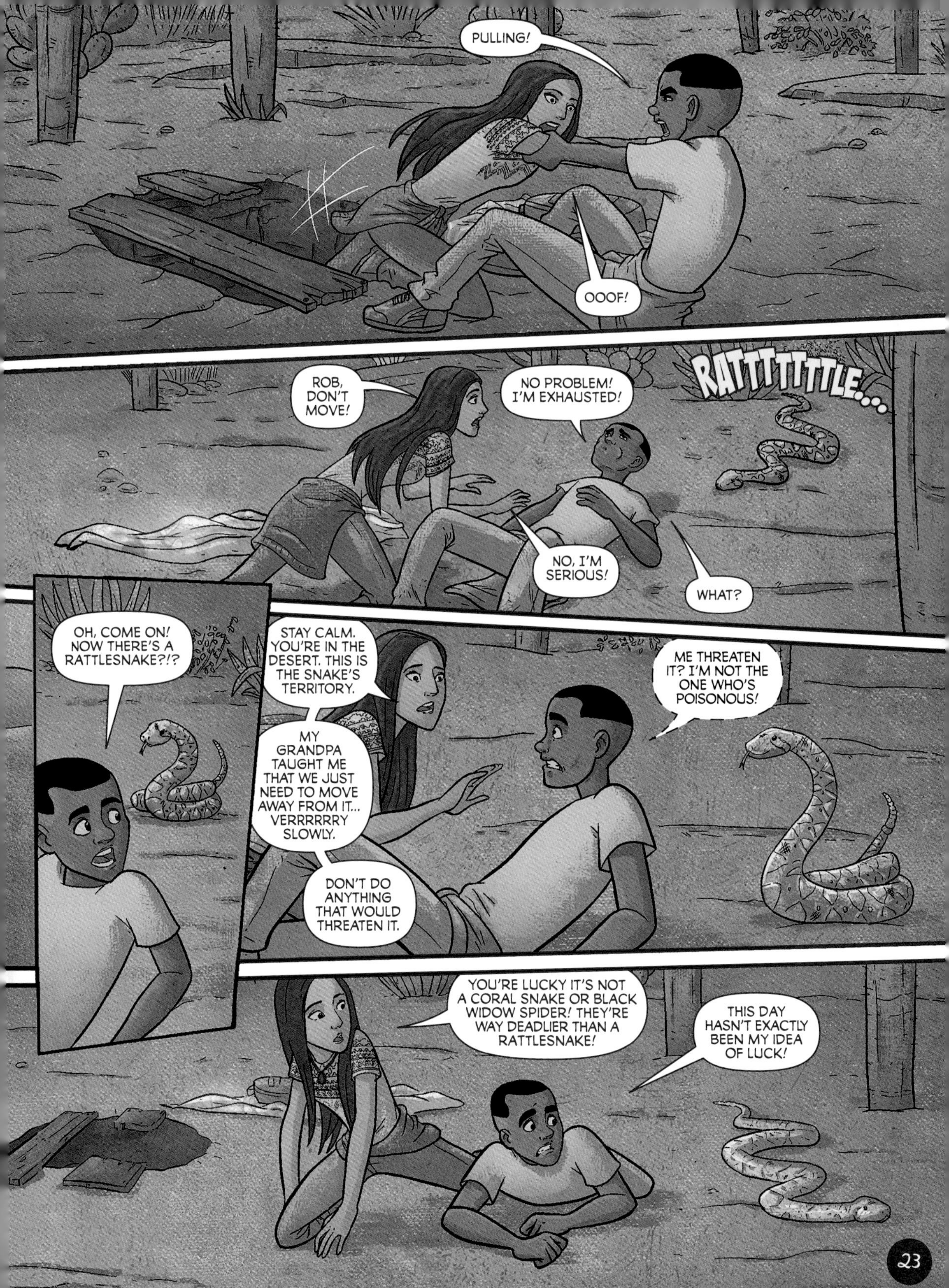
PULLING!
OOOF!
ROB, DON'T MOVE!
NO PROBLEM! I'M EXHAUSTED!
RATTTTTTTLE...
NO, I'M SERIOUS!
WHAT?
OH, COME ON! NOW THERE'S A RATTLESNAKE?!?
STAY CALM. YOU'RE IN THE DESERT. THIS IS THE SNAKE'S TERRITORY.
MY GRANDPA TAUGHT ME THAT WE JUST NEED TO MOVE AWAY FROM IT... VERRRRRRY SLOWLY.
DON'T DO ANYTHING THAT WOULD THREATEN IT.
ME THREATEN IT? I'M NOT THE ONE WHO'S POISONOUS!
YOU'RE LUCKY IT'S NOT A CORAL SNAKE OR BLACK WIDOW SPIDER! THEY'RE WAY DEADLIER THAN A RATTLESNAKE!
THIS DAY HASN'T EXACTLY BEEN MY IDEA OF LUCK!

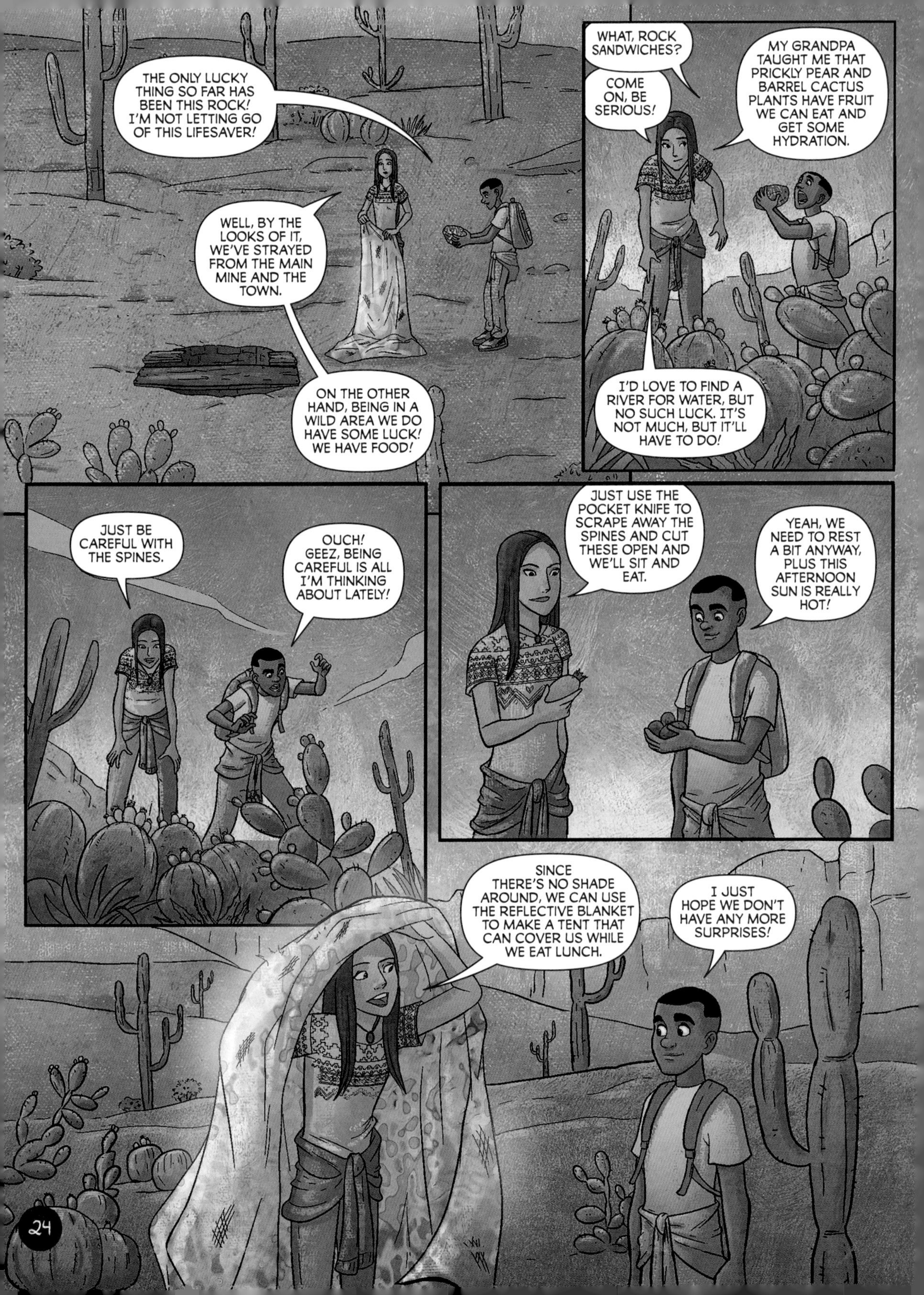

THE ONLY LUCKY THING SO FAR HAS BEEN THIS ROCK! I'M NOT LETTING GO OF THIS LIFESAVER!
WELL, BY THE LOOKS OF IT, WE'VE STRAYED FROM THE MAIN MINE AND THE TOWN.
ON THE OTHER HAND, BEING IN A WILD AREA WE DO HAVE SOME LUCK! WE HAVE FOOD!
WHAT, ROCK SANDWICHES?
COME ON, BE SERIOUS!
MY GRANDPA TAUGHT ME THAT PRICKLY PEAR AND BARREL CACTUS PLANTS HAVE FRUIT WE CAN EAT AND GET SOME HYDRATION.
I'D LOVE TO FIND A RIVER FOR WATER, BUT NO SUCH LUCK. IT'S NOT MUCH, BUT IT'LL HAVE TO DO!
JUST BE CAREFUL WITH THE SPINES.
OUCH! GEEZ, BEING CAREFUL IS ALL I'M THINKING ABOUT LATELY!
JUST USE THE POCKET KNIFE TO SCRAPE AWAY THE SPINES AND CUT THESE OPEN AND WE'LL SIT AND EAT.
YEAH, WE NEED TO REST A BIT ANYWAY, PLUS THIS AFTERNOON SUN IS REALLY HOT!
SINCE THERE'S NO SHADE AROUND, WE CAN USE THE REFLECTIVE BLANKET TO MAKE A TENT THAT CAN COVER US WHILE WE EAT LUNCH.
I JUST HOPE WE DON'T HAVE ANY MORE SURPRISES!

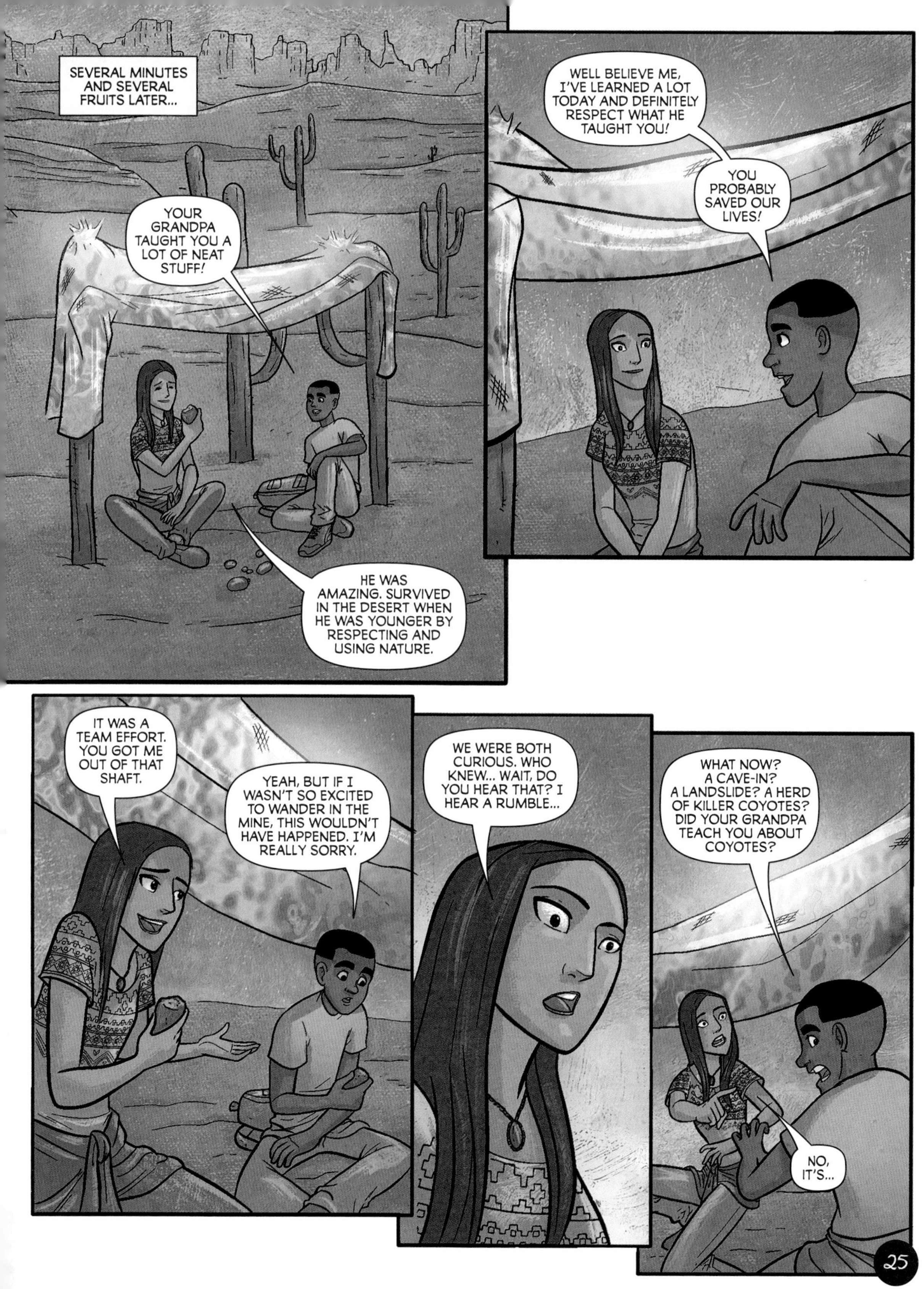
SEVERAL MINUTES AND SEVERAL FRUITS LATER...
YOUR GRANDPA TAUGHT YOU A LOT OF NEAT STUFF!
HE WAS AMAZING. SURVIVED IN THE DESERT WHEN HE WAS YOUNGER BY RESPECTING AND USING NATURE.
WELL BELIEVE ME, I'VE LEARNED A LOT TODAY AND DEFINITELY RESPECT WHAT HE TAUGHT YOU!
YOU PROBABLY SAVED OUR LIVES!
IT WAS A TEAM EFFORT. YOU GOT ME OUT OF THAT SHAFT.
YEAH, BUT IF I WASN'T SO EXCITED TO WANDER IN THE MINE, THIS WOULDN'T HAVE HAPPENED. I'M REALLY SORRY.
WE WERE BOTH CURIOUS. WHO KNEW... WAIT, DO YOU HEAR THAT? I HEAR A RUMBLE...
WHAT NOW? A CAVE-IN? A LANDSLIDE? A HERD OF KILLER COYOTES? DID YOUR GRANDPA TEACH YOU ABOUT COYOTES?
NO, IT'S...

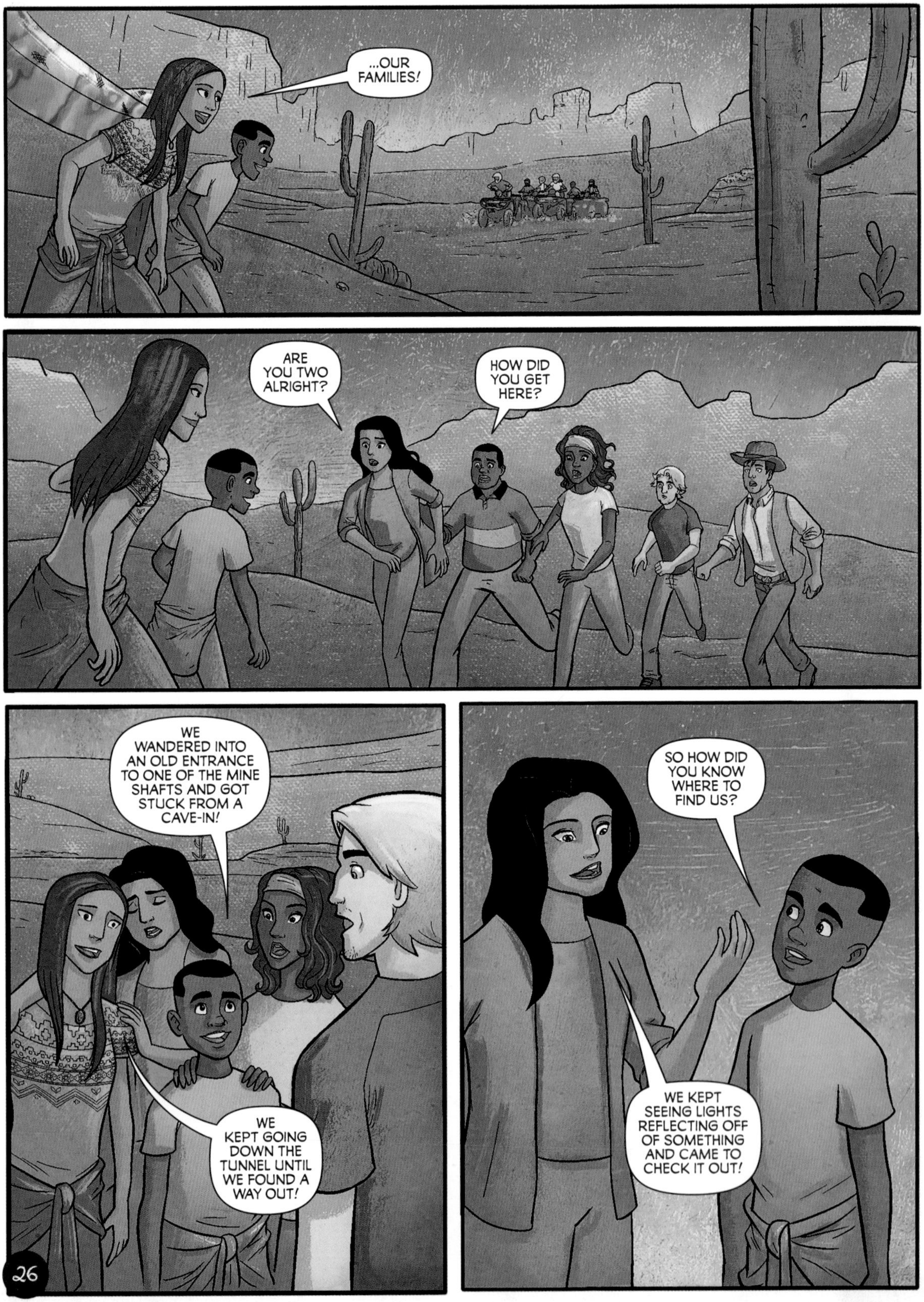
...OUR FAMILIES!
ARE YOU TWO ALRIGHT?
HOW DID YOU GET HERE?
WE WANDERED INTO AN OLD ENTRANCE TO ONE OF THE MINE SHAFTS AND GOT STUCK FROM A CAVE-IN!
WE KEPT GOING DOWN THE TUNNEL UNTIL WE FOUND A WAY OUT!
SO HOW DID YOU KNOW WHERE TO FIND US?
WE KEPT SEEING LIGHTS REFLECTING OFF OF SOMETHING AND CAME TO CHECK IT OUT!

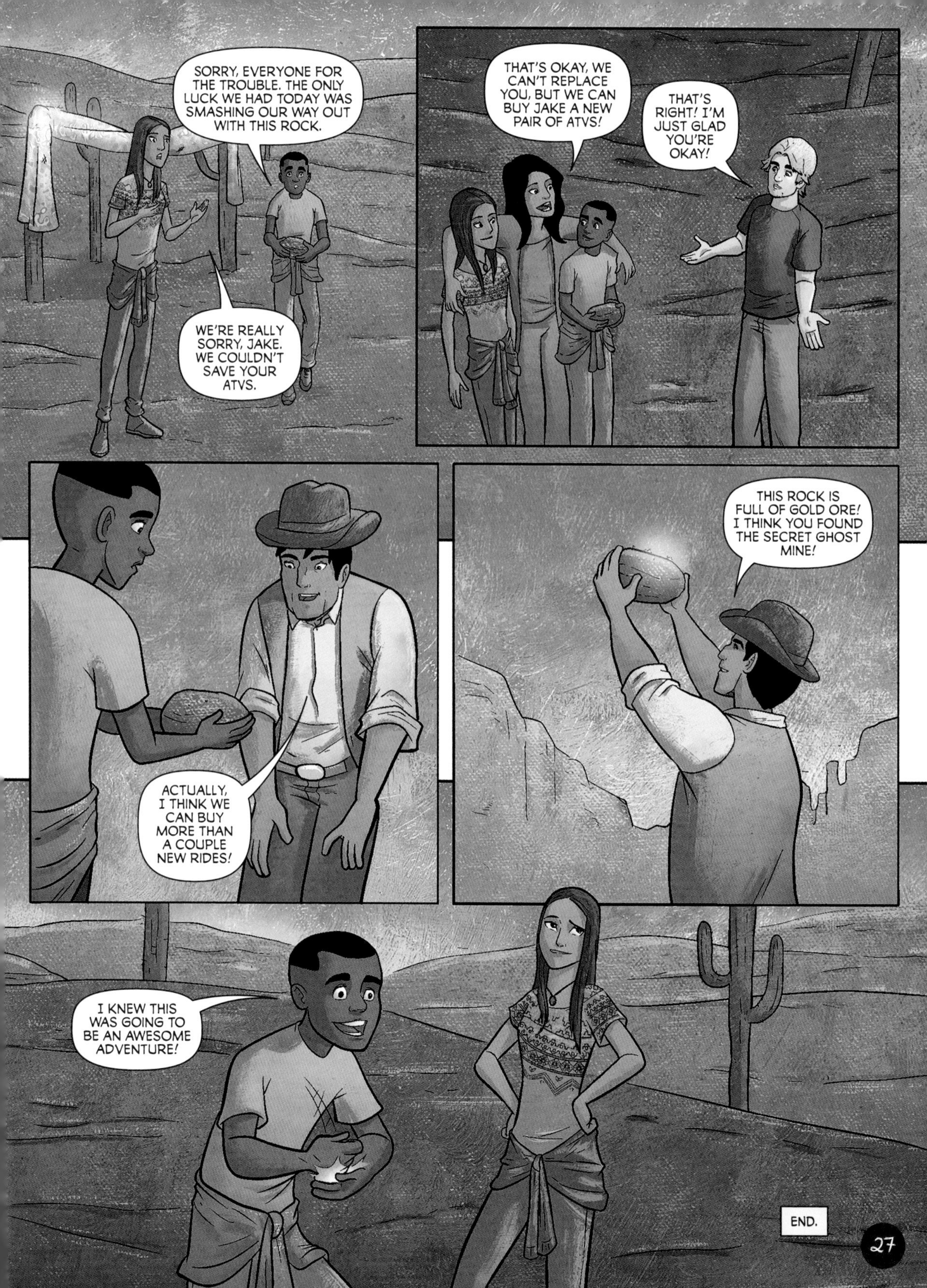

SORRY, EVERYONE FOR THE TROUBLE. THE ONLY LUCK WE HAD TODAY WAS SMASHING OUR WAY OUT WITH THIS ROCK.
WE'RE REALLY SORRY, JAKE. WE COULDN'T SAVE YOUR ATVS.
THAT'S OKAY, WE CAN'T REPLACE YOU, BUT WE CAN BUY JAKE A NEW PAIR OF ATVS!
THAT'S RIGHT! I'M JUST GLAD YOU'RE OKAY!
ACTUALLY, I THINK WE CAN BUY MORE THAN A COUPLE NEW RIDES!
THIS ROCK IS FULL OF GOLD ORE! I THINK YOU FOUND THE SECRET GHOST MINE!
I KNEW THIS WAS GOING TO BE AN AWESOME ADVENTURE!
END.

Desert Survival Guide

The Rule of Three

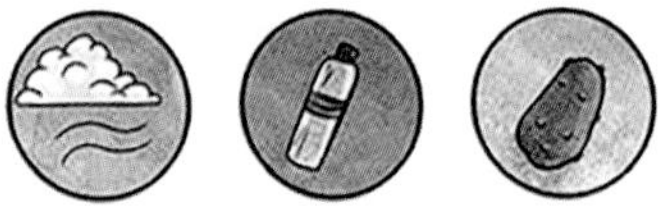

People need air, food, water, and shelter in order to survive. When you're in desperate situations, remember the Rule of Three. Usually, the longest a person should go and still have body function is three minutes without air, three hours without shelter in an extreme environment, three days without water, and three weeks without food. There can be incredible survival stories that differ from these guidelines, but the Rule of Three is a good rule of thumb.

Hello Hydration

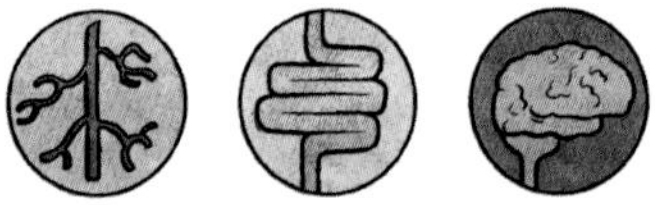

Clean drinking water is critical to human survival. It keeps your blood flowing well, your digestive system working properly, and helps keep your brain focused and alert. The average person needs about half a gallon (2 l) of water a day depending on activity level. When out in nature, try not to drink still or slow-moving water from ponds, lakes, or rivers. Bacteria can easily form in these sources. Small, flowing streams are better as less bacteria forms in these. Collecting rainwater is safest. Collecting moisture using condensation is safe, but not as quick or easy. However, to be safe, always try to filter and boil the water to remove debris and kill bacteria. Boil the filtered water for at least 10 minutes and then cool it down until it is safe to drink.

In the desert, water is often scarce. Dig into the ground near vegetation until water pools at the water table. You can also get emergency hydration from the edible fruits of certain cactus plants. However, be on guard! Plants and the liquids found in them can often cause digestive issues and can lead to quicker dehydration!

No Bite for This Bark

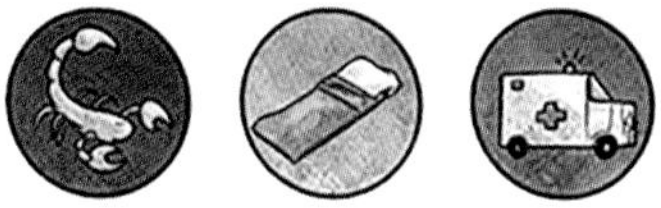

They don't have teeth, but their stingers can hurt! Many types of scorpion live in the southwestern United States. The Arizona bark scorpion's sting is the one that can cause the worst symptoms. These include burning pain, swelling, and numbness. Severe symptoms include muscle twitching, difficulty breathing, high blood pressure, nausea, vomiting, and irregular heart rate. If you are stung, seek medical care immediately. In the meantime, wash the area with soap and water. Apply a cool cloth on for 10 minutes then off for 10 minutes. Keep the affected area in a comfortable position. The sting is rarely fatal to healthy adults, unless untreated. Babies, small children, and the elderly should seek medical care immediately. Those with weakened immune systems and people with allergies to arachnid stings or bites should be careful in areas with scorpions. To avoid contact as much as possible, especially when camping, check sleeping bags, clothes, and shoes by shaking them away from you before use. If you see a scorpion in your home, call an exterminator. They are difficult to eliminate!

If You Hear a Rattle...

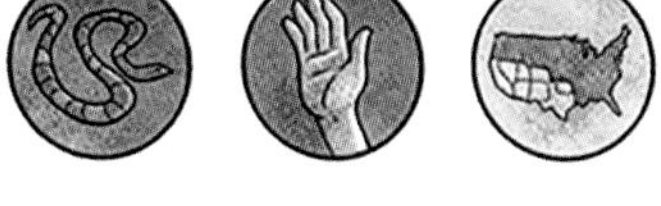

Rattlesnakes and coral snakes are the most dangerous snakes in the southwestern United States. They can't eat humans, so they bite out of fear or self-defense. Coral snakes are more poisonous than rattlesnakes, but they inject less venom. If you come across a snake, back away slowly with non-threatening movements. If you get bitten, seek medical attention immediately. Do not attempt to suck out the venom or put a tourniquet around the area. That could make the injury worse.

What Do You Think?

Exploring can be exciting, but always demonstrate safety and responsibility. It may seem like it's taking the fun away. But it'll actually ensure you can have the most enjoyment!

• Describe a time you were in such a hurry to try something new that you didn't take proper safety precautions. What would you tell someone trying that experience for the first time?

• Why do you think Lillian respected her grandfather's teachings? What have you learned from elders in your life?

• Describe your scariest animal encounter. How did you respond to it? What did you learn that could help someone else?

• What do you think the allure is behind a ghost town? What would you want to see if you visited one?

• Do you think there are positive aspects to mining? What about negative ones? How can we protect the environment and still get what we need?

Desert Survival Trivia

1. There are 13 types of rattlesnakes in Arizona. Be careful if you hear that rattling sound!

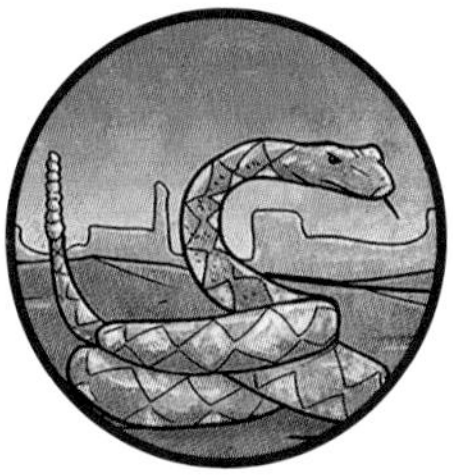

2. Scorpions are generally nocturnal, so be careful at night. Be sure to check your belongings carefully when you wake up in the morning in an infested area!

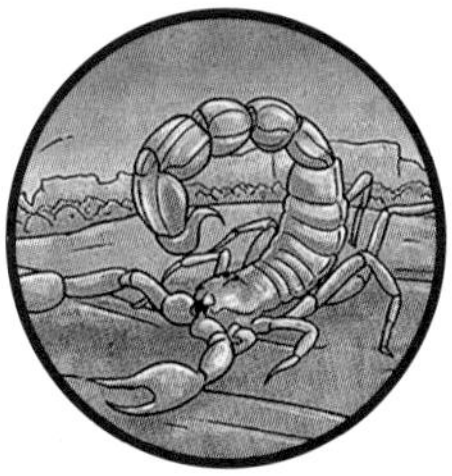

3. The Navajo Native Americans from the regions of Arizona, Utah, and New Mexico served as code talkers during World War II. Because their language was so complex, enemies could not figure out the codes the US Marines were using in the Pacific!

4. Cactus fruit and cactus water are believed to have very healthy and healing properties. But make sure they are processed properly so you don't make yourself sick!

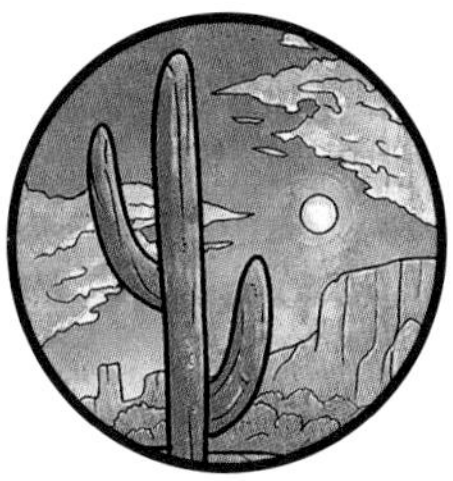

5. ATVs were first made as early as the 1890s as a form of horseless carriage! They became more popular in the 1960s and 1970s as military vehicles. In the 1980s they became recreational vehicles. The most popular versions have three or four wheels, although some military versions have six!

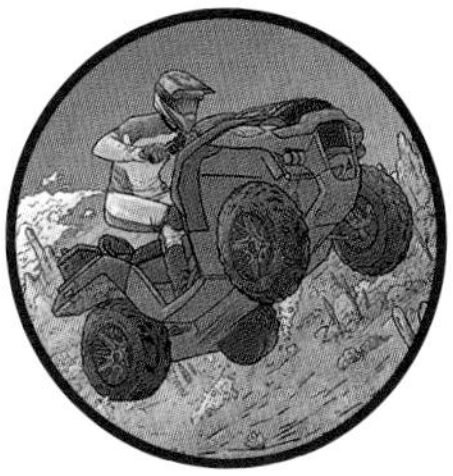

Glossary

- **ATV** – all-terrain vehicle.

- **code talkers** – Native Americans who served in the US armed forces during World War I and World War II. Code talkers developed and used codes in Native American languages to send secret messages.

- **coincidence** – events that happen at the same time by accident, but seem to have some connection.

- **Navajo** (NAH-vuh-hoh) – a Native American people of the southwestern United States.

- **nocturnal** – sleeping during the day and being active at night.

- **reflective** – able to bounce light off of itself.

Online Resources

Booklinks
NONFICTION NETWORK
FREE! ONLINE NONFICTION RESOURCES

To learn more about desert survival, please visit **abdobooklinks.com** or scan this QR code. These links are routinely monitored and updated to provide the most current information available.